SHATTERED

STORIES OF CHILDREN AND WAR

SHATTERED

STORIES OF CHILDREN AND WAR

EDITED BY
JENNIFER ARMSTRONG

ALFRED A. KNOPF ⟍ NEW YORK

THIS IS A BORZOI BOOK PUBLISHED BY ALFRED A. KNOPF

Copyright © 2002 by Jennifer Armstrong
All rights reserved under International and Pan-American Copyright Conventions.
Published in the United States of America by Alfred A. Knopf, a division of Random
House, Inc., New York, and simultaneously in Canada by Random House of
Canada Limited, Toronto. Distributed by Random House, Inc., New York.
KNOPF, BORZOI BOOKS, and the colophon are registered trademarks
of Random House, Inc.

www.randomhouse.com/teens

Library of Congress Cataloging-in-Publication Data:
Shattered : stories of children and war / edited by Jennifer Armstrong
p.   cm.
Contents: The second day / Ibtisam Barakat — Shattered / Marilyn Singer — Bad day
for baseball / Graham Salisbury — I'll see you when this war is over / M. E. Kerr —
Golpe de estado / Dian Curtis Regan — Snap, crackle, pop / Lois Metzger — Things
happen / Lisa Rowe Fraustino — Faizabad harvest, 1980 / Suzanne Fisher Staples —
Sounds of thunder / Joseph Bruchac — Witness / Jennifer Armstrong — War is swell /
David Lubar — Hope / Gloria D. Miklowitz.
ISBN 0-375-81112-5 (trade) — ISBN 0-375-91112-X (lib. bdg.)
1. War stories. [1. War—Fiction. 2. Short stories.] I. Armstrong, Jennifer, 1961–
PZ5 .S5147   2002
[Fic]—dc21   2001018609

Printed in the United States of America
February 2002
10 9 8 7 6 5 4 3 2 1
First Edition

Young commando holding a machine gun. Beirut, Lebanon, 1970.

CONTENTS

Editor's Introduction

My great-grandfather Alfred Armstrong was a corporal in the New York 134th Regiment during the Civil War. He enlisted in Schoharie, New York, at about the same time that my friend Joseph Bruchac's great-grandfather Lewis Bowman enlisted in nearby Saratoga. They didn't serve in the same regiment, but I believe they must have fought in the same division of regiments from upstate New York. My great-grandfather was captured just before the battle of Gettysburg, and was safely out of commission for that bloody engagement, where his regiment lost 63 percent of their men. If Alfred Armstrong hadn't been a prisoner of war in Virginia, I might not be here now. You can read about what happened to Lewis Bowman in Bruchac's story "Sounds of Thunder."

Even so far removed from the Civil War, I shudder to think how few generations separate me from that conflict. How much more painful are the scars and bruises felt by those whose wars are much closer in time—in their parents' lives or in their own? Wars are supposed to be the business of officers and soldiers, but that's not how it happens. Wars welcome everyone with equal enthusiasm. They leave nobody out—not the soldiers' families, not the farmer whose field is used as a battleground, not the children whose school is bombed by distant artillery, not the mother who is trying to keep her family together as they are driven off their land by an approaching army. *Everybody, join in! There's room for all!* According to United Nations reports, armed conflicts now kill and maim *more children* than soldiers. Clearly, war isn't just for soldiers anymore, if, in fact, it ever was. When I was a kid and the Vietnam War was part of the nightly newscast, there was a popular slogan: "War is not healthy for children and other living things." And really, there's no arguing with that one.

The stories in this collection are about kids and teenagers who feel the heavy hand of war in their lives. Some of them are very painful and unsettling to read. Some of them may be bewildering: Where is this? What war is this? When does this take place? What is this war about? But put yourself in the position of the characters in the stories. You are going to school. You have parents, brothers, sisters, friends. You have a normal life—and, suddenly, people you don't know are trying to kill you. Does it matter who they are? Or why they are dropping bombs on your house? Or why they have taken your father? No, it does not matter, because what you must do now is survive. Maybe later you will ask questions. But not now.

Some of the stories are farther from the bombs and the bullets, but they are not any farther from the fear and the destruction. How can that war so far away hurt me? It has nothing to do with me. Those people are no concern of mine. That was a long time ago. So how can it be that my life has suddenly been turned upside down? War has a long reach.

This collection of stories isn't meant to be a history lesson about this war or that revolution. Nor is it intended to be a political manifesto or a pacifist plea. Personally, I think some wars are justified; some wars do have to be fought. But you might think otherwise—many people do. Read "Faizabad Harvest, 1980" by Suzanne Fisher Staples and then "I'll See You When This War Is Over" by M. E. Kerr. Put yourself into those stories and ask if you would act differently. Can war even be a good thing? David Lubar's story, "War Is Swell," imagines how it might be an improvement. Can the rescue of war victims have frightening consequences in later generations? Read "Hope" by Gloria Miklowitz and then "The Second Day" by Ibtisam Barakat. If you feel that you are running in circles, that you don't know what to think, don't be surprised.

Because it's confusing, this thing called war, confusing and hard to think about dispassionately. Wars are as complex and varied as the people who experience them, and they can't be discussed with quick summaries or easy judgments. By exploring war through the idiosyncrasies of story, character, and setting, you may begin to form your own ideas about what war is, what it means, where it comes from, and what happens when it happens. Stories can be a way of looking at reality. We tell stories to help us walk closer to frightening truth, and with something as difficult as war, stories might be the best way to get there. There can't be anything more serious or consequential for people than a war; it has that long reach and heavy hand. When that hand comes down, something—someone—will be shattered.

Jennifer Armstrong
Saratoga Springs, New York

The Second Day

Ibtisam Barakat

Yesterday, as the war finished its first day, we became refugees. The fires, air raids, bullets, and bombardment ruined many homes and burned many crop fields. They drove us away in the middle of the night like a nation of terrified deer. We all knew that someone wanted us dead yesterday. So we ran to the caves and then through the fields that would take us to the second day, and to a road through which we could cross to safety in a neighboring country.

But the road was empty except for the fierce June sun that pierced my face. I asked that I sit. My father instructed that I must remain standing and ready to run. But my feet had gotten bruised from running without shoes yesterday, and I could not stand. When the sun centered in the sky and my noon shadow pooled like the blood of a butchered animal below me, I fell to the ground, asleep. Mother, who hovered over while holding my infant sister to her chest, and my two brothers frantically shook me and pinched my cheeks until I woke up again.

"No one can carry you," Dad explained as he skinned off a piece of cucumber and rubbed it on my face to further awaken me. He had carried the cucumber to replace water at Mother's urging last night.

"Do you really think it can replace water?" he had exclaimed in the darkness before we fled. "I imagine so," she had replied.

"Imagine" was Mother's favorite word. In Arabic, she would say *Batkhayyal,* which also meant "to see the shadow of a thought," as if one is separated from it by a thin cloth. Mother seemed to dwell behind this veil, gaze through it, and long for uniting with its other side. Mother could imagine solutions to many problems and would pop them out of her mouth with the ease I popped my Bazooka chewing gum.

Now, standing only one step away from my mother, I could see that she had slipped into the other side and the door was shut behind her. My heart pounded at the barrier and begged that she come out and see me. But her gaze only floated afar on the horizon. When she finally spoke, the words were not directed at me.

"I hear something in the distance," she said quietly, as if not to disturb the spider-thread perception connecting the sound to her ear, "perhaps an engine."

A fierce look covered my father's face. He closed his eyes, cupped his ears, and opened his mouth, as if to swallow the sound upon capturing it. He asked us all to listen; then he instructed that we hold hands and run behind him.

"If it's a vehicle, I will stop it no matter what that takes," my father vowed.

At the center of the road, Dad flung his arms across his

chest. He was ready to embrace a broad destiny. He wailed after the men to join him, and many answered. Dad and the men huddled and, like magnets, stuck to one another's bodies. They formed a tight-knot barrier. Terror was the mortar that held them together. Their heads faced to the inside, and they looked into one another's eyes to fill each other with courage. Everyone seemed to understand the strategy, and in no time other men formed new knots along the road. The noise now became increasingly louder, its diesel hum madly goading everyone's desperate hopes and deepest worries.

People spoke words of solid anger as they fought to get closer to the road. They pushed and propelled one another in every direction, like marble balls in a child's play. My brothers and I knew to plant our bodies where we could see our dad: We were a compass needle, and he was our North. Our mother, a tall and astonishingly strong woman who relied on her hands more than she ever relied on words, was always behind us and making certain we stood ahead of the crowd.

It was a white water tanker that emerged from the silver spot on the horizon. People cried out to God in gratitude and jumped high in the air as if to deliver the words. But the tanker increased its speed as it approached a group of men that blocked the road. They all dashed to the side at the last moment, and the tanker went through like a comb parting hair.

The tanker then came closer to Dad and the barricade of men that formed with him. The men raised their voices and promised that the tanker would not go through. They chanted that God is mightiest. They asked for His help, which seemed to be as near as the end of the heart-wrenching screech that brought the tanker to a stop. Dad dropped to the ground in immediate prayer; the men formed a circle to protect him.

Quickly, people stuck themselves to the tanker like ants on an abandoned candy bar. Men climbed on the tank. Women, almost all of them carrying children, cried as it was apparent that the tanker could not transport all of us. Mother instructed that my brothers and I must respond to all of her directions at a bullet's speed. The three of us, who had become more like soldiers than children that day, nodded our heads in compliance.

The directions were given upon hearing Dad's voice, which came to us shredded by noises. But Mother could understand every word. Dad was asking us to move closer to the tanker's door. Mother immediately commanded that my brothers climb up the tanker, find a way to fling their bodies on the windshield, and block the driver's view. She then pulled me up by the arm and ordered that I squeeze myself among the bodies or, if I must, seep through them like water, but get myself to stand on the doorstep of the tanker, hold its handle, and not let go. She said she would be right behind me and watch each of my steps.

I did not know how, but my brothers sliced through every-thing and ended up on the windshield, and I took myself to the door's handle. People pushed me off repeatedly, but I climbed up on their clothes and everything my hands could touch until I held a piece of the handle. I pressed my face fiercely against the window and waited for my mother to reach me with her voice. When she then called my name, I could see that she'd been right behind me and had been supporting my weight with her body to keep me on the step.

Looking inside, I saw the driver, his wife, and three children. They were piled up on one another and were looking at all of the mad faces that surrounded them. I also saw my father's face pressed against the opposite window. He was unleashing a stream of curses that pinned the driver to his seat. He was asking the driver to let us inside with his family, and let men hang on to the tanker for the journey to Jordan. If the driver wouldn't accept, my father threatened that the men would shoot the tanker's tires.

The driver pleaded that he could not open the door lest people force him and his family out of the seat and then take the tanker and leave. But Dad promised that this would not happen. The driver hesitated until we all heard the howling of renewed bombardment.

Heads were swinging in all directions to determine where the sounds came from when the driver beckoned to his wife and she opened the door. My mother, my brothers, and I instantly swirled around the door and shoved ourselves into the seat. The driver's children cried. His wife looked into my mother's face and cursed somberly. But Mother remained silent. She only reached to the door and locked it.

The driver recited short prayers, then announced that we

United Nations Relief and Works Agency data showed more than would be moving nonstop until we crossed the border to Jordan. I did not know how long that would take us but hoped for a short time in the tanker. My feet, with their bruises that pushed against my mother's back, pulsed madly. My head was pressed against the glass of the tiny window behind the seat.

Once again, my father was on the other side of the glass. This time he was holding a metal peg with which he knocked twice at the tank. He screamed to the driver that two knocks would be the signal to slow down so the men wouldn't fall off, and three knocks the signal to stop. The driver agreed.

The scattered sounds of bombardment made me jump involuntarily each time. They also made the driver increase his speed. But each time he did, men slowed him down by knocking twice. He alternated his answer to them with curses and prayers for the time when he would separate from all of us in peace.

The men also burst into clamor each time a plane zoomed above us. When that happened, their voices swelled and engulfed us. I could feel their voices go through my body like a giant wave that pounded me and left me soaked in anxiety. But I kept my eyes on my father, who had become the only solid center of my seeing. I saw him speak with a man who had a gun. I saw the man take off his gun and hand it to my father. And I then saw my father point to the sky and fire at the war planes that were flickering with their blood-red lights above us.

The driver beeped the horn ragingly; then he stopped and begged my father to halt his bravery. My dad returned the gun to the man who had given it to him and banged on the tank frantically.

"Your man is a lunatic," the driver told my mother.

She argued that Dad knew exactly what he was doing.

The teeming tanker rattled as it toiled to cling to the road. When we got to Jericho, the driver raised his weary voice to warn us from bolting through the glass as he negotiated the steep curves, and my mother and the driver's wife now spoke of dear things they had left behind in Ramallah, where we lived, and Nablus, where the driver's family came from. The driver's wife then invited Mother to visit her sometime when the war was over and when we all returned home. "Bring your children and come spend a day," she said. Now, cloaked in the warm, womanly voices, and calmed by the tanker's rocking motion, I fell asleep.

I woke up when the tanker came to a stop as we approached the border. A patrol soldier told us that we'd arrived in Jordan. The driver flung the tanker's door open and jumped to the ground. He kneeled in prayer. Many men slipped off the tanker and joined him.

"There are air raids on all fronts, and we don't know what will happen and when and where the war will stop," the soldier continued. He directed us to the town of Zarqa, one hour away. He said there were shelters in Zarqa and that many families were opening their homes to receive us. My mother and the driver's wife wept upon hearing this.

whom were still living in refugee camps. The question of

"There is still good in the world," Mother said.

"God does not forget anyone," the driver's wife affirmed.

At the shelter's door in Zarqa, the driver, my dad, and the other men said they must leave us and go to volunteer their help. The driver asked his wife not to worry about him, and my father, who now sat beside the driver, told Mother he would find a way to send us a word at every chance he got. He held out an arm, and my two brothers and I hung from it. When the tanker moved, Dad kept his arm held out far outside of the window for us to see it until the tanker disappeared.

The shelter was a three-story stone house. Before we entered, Mother told the driver's wife that she was uncertain whether my infant sister, whom Mother had been carrying all day, was still breathing. "She's been silent for so long, and I can't get myself to find out if she's alive," she said.

Without words, the driver's wife reached with her hand to my sister's nose. She pinched and held it briefly. To our stunned surprise, my sister coughed and then cried.

We fought our way into the shelter, which was nothing but a sardine-jammed house of strangers. But at the sound of sirens, the crowd quickly swirled into a soup of terrified faces. The sirens were dagger-sharp noises that frequently stabbed through the windows, then through our hearts. They unnerved us and forced everyone to incessantly run up and down the stairs, and come down howling news about fires and bombings they saw from the second- and third-floor windows.

The sirens were warnings before or after bombardment, and they were always followed by a silent moment of nauseating anticipation. My mother and two brothers, the driver's wife, and her children all joined in the stair mania. I hung on to my brothers and hopped along until I could no longer tolerate the pain of being elbowed or shoved or having someone step on my bare feet.

I decided to sit in the corner of the basement. And there, standing almost invisibly in a cloud of dark and quietness, I found a baby donkey. I named him Souma, and that made me forget everything for a moment. I raised my arms and touched Souma's face; he remained still. I spoke with him; he looked at me and listened. I kneeled on the ground and pulled him toward me. He did not resist. And I embraced him with all of my body.

Now, calmed on the inside by the close company of Souma, I could see that the second day had come to a close and left us prisoners in the shelter. The night had already dropped down its thick, impenetrable curtains. The fear of being burned by bombardment had hardened into coal in our hearts. And the piercing sirens made certain we understood that we could not leave the shelter before the war ended.

But we don't know how long this war will last. And tomorrow, the third day is coming. It's only a few hours away from our shelter. It's heading toward us like an armed robber. We don't know what it will take away from us and whom it will injure or kill when it arrives thirsty at sunrise. We don't know how our lives will be altered. We can only imagine.

Shattered

Marilyn Singer

"The air whines and howls. A line of bullets strafes the dust, *zip zip zip*, as if they were staples tacking the brown ground in place. A bomb hits one hut, then another. They explode, sparks blossoming into the air, bright as the hibiscus flowers that once grew nearby—"

"What kind of a bomb?" Teddy asks.

Thea frowns. He's been begging her to do the Story, even though Mom and Dad will be home soon, and here he is interrupting. She feels like yelling, I don't know what kind of damn bomb. I don't *care* what kind of damn bomb! We're getting too old for this. *I'm* getting too old.

But there's already too much damn yelling in the house. Teddy doesn't need more of it. He's got enough problems already.

What was it today? Those rotten kids at school tormenting him again? The ones who call him Turdy and laugh at how he can't swing a bat because he can't play for crap. That nasty teacher Mrs. Exner, who ridicules his compositions in class, the one who's probably even now bad-mouthing him to their folks at Open School Night? He knows more about math than she'll ever know, but he still can't write a sentence that isn't gibberish. Mom has taken him to doctor after doctor. They bandy words like *syndrome* and *cognitive dysfunction* as if they are talking about what to have for lunch. "It's all in his head," Dad said. "It's in his *genes*," Mom snapped back. "No, that's his butt," Dad replied, deadpan. His kind of a joke. Thea laughed. She often laughs whether she finds the jokes funny or not. Dad never joins in.

She looks at Teddy. He's waiting patiently for the answer to his question. That irritates her even more. Sometimes he's as patient as a saint. Sometimes he's as jittery as a parrot in a cage, walking back and forth, twisting his head this way and that. Sometimes she even prefers him that way. "Napalm," she says, dredging up the word from a movie she saw.

"Un-uh. I don't think so," he counters, more thoughtful than sarcastic. "Napalm burns things, but it doesn't explode them."

Then why ask me? she thinks. And how did he know? Probably saw something on the Internet. Teddy was better on the Net than with books he could hold in his hands.

"I meant 'burst into flame,'" she replies—smoothly, she hopes—and continues, "All around is noise, heat, explosion.... But we are in a circle of light—"

"Golden light," Teddy corrects, and this time she doesn't mind.

"Golden light. We are safe. We are safe. Holding hands in the circle of golden light..."

He snuggles closer on their parents' bed—the Story only

really works when it's told in this place of power—and takes her hand. His is broader than it was only, what, a month ago, since they last played the game. Teddy's going to be a big guy someday, Thea thinks, listening to the silence outside the room. *Like Dad*. It's the only thing he and Teddy have in common. That, and perhaps their smile, but Thea has rarely seen her father's. Except in the photograph. The one in the Book. There's Dad and his army buddies in Da Nang, Thea pictures them. Two died a few days later. And they're all smiling, Dad biggest of all. A smile that says, I know just who I am here. Ain't war grand?

Teddy yawns and shifts. There is a fresh bruise on his right arm. What *did* happen in school today? Thea touches the bruise lightly. Teddy winces. Thea guesses it was not because she's hurt him but because he is worried she'll ask him about it. He talks about pain as little as their father. Perhaps they are more alike than she thought. She lies quietly next to him then until his breathing gets deeper and more regular. Then she gets up and leaves the room.

Dad's studio is in back of the house, a separate small building with benches and cabinets and sheets and sheets of glass that he makes into elegant dinnerware and surprising hangings. Every year at the local craft fairs where Thea helps to sell his wares, a classmate or three says, "Oh, wow, I didn't know your dad's a glassblower." "He's not," she always replies. "He doesn't blow glass, he fuses it." Thea works with him, when he lets her, cutting out strips and squares of glass, taping them together to lay in a mold, turning on the kiln to

Orange over jungle areas to kill the leaves that could conceal make them melt and fuse. She knows she's pretty good at it, but she'll never be as good as her father. Teddy's hands look like their father's, but he'll never be any good at all. Dad's hands are quick, steady, strong. Equally at ease with a stained-glass window or a rifle, a fact that has never struck Thea as contradictory.

She crosses to the kiln. It is cooling down, but still quite warm. Earlier she and Dad loaded it with bowls, one of them Thea's. She's been working on a new pattern—delicate bursts of iridescent color in a field of snow-white glass. It's for Mom's birthday. Dad calls it "Prism." Thea calls it "Firefight"—though she'd never tell him that. She believes that the skirmishes he was in must have had their own strange beauty—flashes of light blooming like chrysanthemums against a brighter sun, streaking like meteors in the night sky. Even the sweat-streaked coffee, cream, honey, root-beer bodies of the men in their drab fatigues were beautiful—something familiar, defined, vital in that jungly place. Her dad has never told her that. But she's seen it in the Book: his scrapbook—the photos and letters he showed her and Teddy exactly once. The pictures weren't blood-and-guts, but they scared Teddy. He had nightmares for weeks. Mom was furious. "You ever show him that stuff again, we're out of here," she blasted. *That* scared Thea. And that night the Story was born, a secret comfort to be shared with only her brother. Every now and then, to get inspiration, she looks at the Book again. She knows where it's hidden—in a small cubbyhole behind sheets of glass. She needs to look at it now.

enemy guerrillas. During the 1990s, government studies showed

Behind the glass in front of the cubbyhole is a small water-color of hibiscus flowers, the only thing her dad has kept from the "worthless" art class he took in college. He didn't paint it. Some girl named Marie did. There's a picture of her, blond and freckled, in the scrapbook. She's rubbing Dad's newly shorn head. The caption beneath says, in foreign, feminine hand-writing, "Hey, soldier! Marie and Tom, 1969."

At times, Thea has wondered what happened to Marie. All she knows, all that Dad has said about her, is that years ago she married a doctor and moved to Idaho. "Good for her," Mom said. Thea couldn't tell whether she was glad for Marie or just glad she was gone. Thea cannot picture her mother ever painting flowers. "Two left thumbs," she says, sounding proud of it, an attitude Thea will never understand.

Pushing aside the painting, Thea reaches inside the cubbyhole for the Book. It isn't there. She jerks back her hand in shock, then plunges it in deeper, connecting at last with the nubbly imitation-leather spine. Someone's looked at it recently and pushed it farther back than usual. Dad? she wonders. She has no idea how often he looks at his scrap-book. It's always been in the same exact spot she's careful to leave it.

Sitting down at the desk, she glances at her dad's latest screensaver—flying $1,000 bills zipping across the computer monitor—and opens the book. She flips past Marie, whom she doesn't need to see today, maybe ever, really, as well as pictures of Dad and his buddies at boot camp, to the photos of Vietnam. She studies the images of the men, the trees, the

that the children of veterans who had been exposed to Agent

buildings. Some of the pictures are posed, some not at all. All of them are so concrete. At last she allows herself to turn to the back of the book. Under a photo of a quiet field in which stand an old man and a water buffalo flicking its ears at an invisible swarm of flies, in a hollow dug into the cover, a spent cartridge is taped. There is a date, but no caption. Of all the images in the book, this is the one that frightened Teddy the most. Sometimes he's as dense as a water buffalo himself, but at age three, he understood a thing it took Thea longer to realize: Someone, someplace, sometime did, would, was going to be—shattered.

Thea stares at the picture for a long time, so lost in thought that she does not hear the studio door open. She jumps when Teddy says, "Thea, I had an accident."

He's standing there in a different pair of pajama bottoms with a bundle of linen in his arms.

"Oh, damn," she growls. She shouldn't have let him fall asleep in their parents' room. But he hasn't wet the bed in such a long time she thought he was over it.

"What are you looking at?" he asks, lumbering toward the desk, trailing sheets and blankets behind him.

"Nothing," Thea says, and slaps the book shut.

"Is that Dad's war book?"

"No," she lies, and frowns. Could it be? Could Teddy be the mystery mover?

He ignores her and barrels around the desk with a sur-prising burst of speed, not really fast, but quicker than she expects—like a tortoise that's got its eye on some appetizing

Orange had higher-than-normal rates of birth defects and were lettuce. He flips open the Book to the back page and fingers the shell.

"Go do the laundry. Now!" she barks.

He backs away. "I don't know how to use the washing machine."

"I showed you last week."

"I forgot," he replies simply.

Of course he has. "Oh, for God's sake, Teddy," she snaps. "You are useless!"

His eyes cloud with hurt. It's worse than a punch in the stomach. But there's no time to apologize, not if she wants to prevent an even worse mood than Open School Night is sure to bring. She grabs the damp, reeking laundry. "Where's the pad? You have to wash the pad, too." Now her voice is also quaking.

Teddy sighs. "I'll get it."

Too late. Dad's voice is outside the studio door.

"Damn it! Where is that kid? I'm tired of sleeping in piss."

The ridiculous image of draping themselves with the sheets and pretending they're furniture comes into Thea's head—the way people do in stupid old comedies. Instead, she and Teddy just freeze in place.

Their father bangs in, still in his hat and coat. "Doctors! Teachers! I don't want to hear about any more of those freakin' idiots."

"Tom," warns their mother, right at his heels. She hasn't even taken off her gloves. This is bad, Thea thinks. Mom does not usually follow Dad into the studio unless invited. It's his den, his space, his sanctuary.

Dad is too revved up to stop. "His bladder and his brain, they're both the size of a pea. Of a pee!"

"Tom!" Mom yells. She's staring at her children.

Dad sees them, too, at the exact same moment. Sees the desk behind them with the still-open book.

Tick, tick, Thea hears. It's coming from Dad's Felix the Cat clock, but Thea imagines that the Book is a bomb about to explode.

Then Teddy, low and plaintive, says, "I could learn to shoot a gun."

Before Dad can roar, "Like hell you could," before Thea can ask, "But you don't want to, do you?" Mom rushes across the room and grabs the Book. Before anyone can stop her, she yanks open the kiln, tosses it inside, and slams the door shut.

"*No!*" Thea shouts, outracing her father to push aside her mother, hoping the laws of thermodynamics will somehow be suspended, that she won't find what she knows she will. And does: the Book in flames and her beautiful "Firefight" cracked, along with every other piece in the kiln.

"My bowl!" she wails. Or is it, "My Book"? Even Thea isn't sure. Her voice rises like a high, thin wind above Dad's bellows of rage and Mom's crackles of anguished justification. "You had no right....He didn't show it to us. He *never* showed it to us," Thea wails.

Suddenly, she's hitting her mother's arms, flailing at her father's chest. Hitting and swearing and sobbing until Dad pulls her against him, holding her tightly, letting her tears settle into a deeper grief.

"Oh, God," Mom whispers. "Oh, God. I'm sorry. I'm so sorry." She touches Thea's arm. Thea's skin twitches. She turns her head away from Mom's face and hand, and remembers Teddy. Where is he?

She sees him over by the kiln, wearing one of Dad's thick gloves, slowly opening the door to survey the destruction. Breaking free of her father and mother, she moves to his side. "Teddy, be careful," she says.

Silently, he takes her hand. She lets him. The glow from the kiln pours out, enveloping them in a golden circle of light.

Bad Day for Baseball

Graham Salisbury

"Masa. Hey, Masa."

Someone shook my shoulder. I rolled away, trying to hang on to my dream. There was a storm, rain and thunder—loud thunder. I was on a fishing boat.

"Masa, wake up. Butchie's on the phone."

The dream fell apart. The image of the boat scattered, and the rain stopped...but the thunder was still there, louder now.

"Masa, get up!"

I rolled back and squinted up at my younger brother.

He nudged me again.

"Kay-okay. Jeez."

My dog, Zippy, jumped up on my bed and licked my face. I shoved him away. "Ho, dog, you got bad breath."

I fumbled for the clock. I had a baseball game at ten. "Cripes, Eldon, it ain't even eight."

"Butchie said get you up."

I shook my head, trying to clear my brain. There was still so much thunder. No...not thunder. Something else, a crumping sound.

In 1942, following the Japanese attack on Pearl Harbor,

"What's all that noise?"

"Army maneuvers."

"How come it's so loud?"

"Dad's outside watching the planes."

"He always does that."

"Come on, Masa, Butchie's waiting."

"Yeah, yeah."

Butchie was my cousin, two years older than me, in his first year at the University of Hawaii, or UH, as we called it. We were like brothers, me and Butchie. I stumbled out to the phone in the kitchen.

"What?" I said.

"Get dressed. I coming to get you. And don't bring that mutt."

"What are you talking about? I can't go anywhere. I got a game today. And anyway, why can't I bring Zippy?"

"Just get dressed. Hurry it up."

"But I—"

"You got a Rotsie uniform? Put it on." He said "Rotsie," not the letters—ROTC, for Reserve Officer Training Corps.

What was he talking about, ROTC?

"I only got the shirt."

"Put it on. And hurry. I'm not kidding, Masa. Don't you see all that smoke?"

"What smoke?"

"The smoke. Look outside."

"Wait," I said.

I glanced out the window. The blue morning sky was

pockmarked with small dirty black puffs. Maneuvers. Eldon was right. But it was probably navy, since it was so close to Honolulu Harbor. "Yeah, I see it, but that's just—"

"No, no, Masa, I telling you. This is for real. Those are Japanese planes out there, and they're bombing us. The radio said for all Rotsie guys go UH, now! So get ready. I coming to get you."

Japanese planes? "But, Butchie—"

He hung up.

I peeked out at the sky one more time. A plane raced by, fast. It was amber, not silver. A sick feeling surged through my stomach. Butchie's wrong, has to be. I ran back to my room and dug up my high school ROTC shirt. I put it on, wrinkled as a rag.

"Eldon, tell Mama I had to go somewhere," I said, hurrying back out to the kitchen. "Where is she, anyway?"

Eldon shrugged, looking worried. "What's going on?"

"Is Dad still outside?"

Eldon pointed his chin toward the front-room window. Out on the street, I could see Dad standing with his hands on his hips, eyes to the sky. Mits Yumoto's dad was gawking next to him.

Zippy leaped at the door, ready to go. "You gotta stay home this time, Zip. Sorry."

I cracked open the door and tried to squeeze out. "Find Mama, Eldon. Something bad is going on. That's not maneuvers."

Eldon hurried out of the kitchen.

"Civilian Exclusion Order." It was believed that Japanese

"Tell her to stay inside!" I called.

Zippy started yelping.

"Kay-okay, Zip. Stop, already. I be back soon."

I shut the door and stuck my fingers under it so he could smell me one last time, his paws scraping the floor. I hated leaving him. He always went with me on Butchie's putt-putt motorbike.

"Dad," I called, running out into the street. "You gotta get inside."

He ignored me, still staring at the sky.

Mr. Yumoto turned and checked out my wrinkled ROTC shirt. He didn't smile.

"Chee," Dad said, "I never seen the army make it so real. Look, this time they even painted the planes like Japanese."

There were fighters all over the place. You could see them filling the sky above the rooftops—circling, hiding behind scattered clouds, then popping out of them and diving, shooting, dropping bombs, and groaning back up with smoky explosions bursting all around them. A sudden wave of biting pinpricks crawled all over my skin. Japanese fighters, swarming like hornets.

"It's ... it's not maneuvers, Dad. Butchie just called. Those really are Japanese planes, and those are real bombs. Can't you hear them?"

Dad turned and frowned at me. I think he was starting to figure it out but didn't want to believe it, either. Not Japan. Not his own country, not his homeland. Never.

"Dad, go inside. You could get hurt out here."

Americans were a threat to national security, and so more than

He didn't move. Stubborn old rock.

I mashed my lips. One good blast nearby and he'll run like a roach in the light.

"Dad, I gotta go with Butchie. They calling for all Rotsie guys to go UH.... Where's Mits?" I asked Mr. Yumoto.

"Fishing. He went down by Kewalo early this morning."

Mits was his son, also a freshman at the university. And like Butchie, he was in ROTC. "You gotta tell him the army wants him to go to the university."

Mr. Yumoto nodded and hurried off.

The sky was getting dirtier, and it wasn't just from the small puffs. Now there were towering stacks of black smoke boiling up from somewhere on the other side of downtown.

A fighter blasted by, just over our heads. I ducked. Dad covered his ears. How could it be? It was impossible. Japan was too far away. But I could see it with my own eyes, the red suns on the wings.

Just then, Butchie screeched up on his smoky motorbike. "Jump on!" he shouted. "Hurry!"

"Dad—"

"Masa, we gotta go!"

I slid on the back and grabbed hold of Butchie's ROTC uniform belt loops. The exhaust pipe was hot against my leg.

Dad walked farther out into the street to get a better look at the planes.

"Uncle," Butchie said, calling to him.

But Dad wouldn't take his eyes off the sky.

Butchie scowled, then gunned the motorbike and flew on

one hundred and twenty thousand people of Japanese ancestry, out of there, heading up toward the university, nestled up in the green valley at the foot of the mountains.

We passed through the city streets, people milling all over the place, everyone looking at the sky. We raced up Ward Avenue, higher and higher, Butchie's motorbike slowing and straining as the road got steeper.

The higher we got, the more we could see, and what we saw was where the smoke was coming from: the navy base. Down over the sweep of trees and rooftops that fell to the sea behind us, you could see at the bottom huge funnels of ugly black smoke, with hungry flames licking the decks of sinking ships in the burning mess that was Pearl Harbor.

People were everywhere. Most out in the streets. Some in their small red-dirt yards. A few standing on top of their cars, everyone silently watching the planes rip into the gray ships that sat like sleeping seagulls on the silvery water.

There was an explosion on the bushy hillside nearby. It startled Butchie and he swerved, nearly sending us into a ditch.

Butchie got control again and cranked the motorbike all out. We leaned forward, trying to make it go faster. I peeked around him, squinting into the wind. Low houses raced by on the right, a rise of mountains on the left.

"Butchie, what we going do?" I yelled over the screaming engine. "I'm only high school Rotsie."

"Don't matter."

"But—"

"Nobody cares right now."

Up and up, racing into the early morning sun, zipping past Roosevelt High School, and across to Punahou, where we turned up again and took a shortcut through a lush, tree-lined street. Even there, with all their big cars and two-story homes, people were out on their porches. Through plate glass windows behind them, I could see huge mirrors and paintings on the walls, and vases stuffed with flowers.

One guy stared at us zipping by. Maybe it was our uniforms, I don't know, but he definitely didn't like what he saw.

I held on tight to Butchie as he swerved and bounced down a narrow road. His ROTC shirt was clean and pressed sharp as brand-new. All I had on was my wrinkled shirt and some old pants with no belt, and nothing on my feet.

At the university there were guys all over the place, hurrying down from cars and bikes parked any which way under the trees and on the grass. We jumped off the motorbike and leaned it against a rock wall, then ran to the football field where everyone was assembling, a hundred of us, maybe more.

Five real army men with grim faces were madly inserting firing pins into the old .30-caliber Springfield rifles that the ROTC used for marching. As they finished, they handed them out with live ammunition.

One guy called to us. "Hey, you! Over here!"

He threw each of us four clips of bullets and a rifle. And he didn't ask if I even knew how to use it. Which I didn't.

I staggered back when I caught the Springfield. It was heavy, way heavier than I thought it would be, and it was

"excluded" from the general population and forced to move into

almost as tall as me. I'd seen them before but had never held one. In high school we used fake wooden rifles. The Springfield made me nervous, even to touch it. What if it was loaded and went off?

"Here," Butchie said, showing me his rifle. "This is where the clip goes. You crank the bolt like this to send a bullet into the chamber. And this is the safety. You can't use the rifle with the safety on. But don't take it off until you need to shoot it."

I fumbled with the clips, stuffing three in my pockets. I dropped the other one in the dirt, picked it up and blew off the dust, then managed to cram it in place in the Springfield. Forget the safety. I didn't want to mess with it. I had never in my life fired a rifle, not even a BB gun. What was I supposed to shoot, anyway? The planes?

I looked up. They were gone now, the sky strangely empty. No buzzing. No screaming engines or flashing wings. I noticed my fingers were trembling.

When everyone had rifles and bullets, the top army guy told us to line up. I recognized Benji Muramoto, and Jiro Ono from my high school, and a couple more guys I didn't know. But that was all. Everyone else was UH ROTC.

"Listen up," the army guy said. His nameplate read CAPT. SMITH. "We're under attack. We don't know what will come next. Anything can happen. We've received word that the Japanese have dropped paratroopers in the mountains and that they're working their way down into the city."

He turned and swept his hand toward the ragged

internment camps for the duration of the war. People were

ridgeline above St. Louis Heights. "They're somewhere up there."

The sun was hot on my face. My stomach knotted up. A coppery, sour taste rose in my throat. This was getting too real.

"We're going to keep them from advancing. That's our job. Is that clear?"

"Yes sir!" all us guys said at the same time, just like in ROTC at school. Only now nobody was laughing or joking around or whispering how stupid it was. At school, ROTC was a joke. But not now, it wasn't.

"And make sure you don't shoot each other, all right?"

He studied our faces, as if he wasn't so sure of us.

"Now listen," he went on. "Most of you boys are Japanese, and if you come face to face with one of these paratroopers, he's going to look like you. I don't know how you're going to feel about that, but I want you to remember this—you are Americans, and these paratroopers will not be your friends. They'll shoot you in a blink. Remember that. They will kill you."

I peeked over at Butchie, who was scowling.

"All right, let's go!" Captain Smith said. He broke us up into platoons of ten and sent us toward the jungled ridge, all of us running into the trees, hunched over like any minute someone hiding in there would shoot at us. Lucky for me, I got to stay with Butchie, who knew how to shoot back if we had to.

He clomped into the woods ahead of me, running parallel

to Manoa Stream. Crazy, I know, but what I was thinking more than getting shot at was how those ROTC boots he had on must be killing his feet. I didn't know how he could even wear them. Me and him both went barefoot almost every day of our lives.

But he wasn't complaining.

The valley was dense and green, a jungle of vines, grass, bushes, and trees—Chinese banyan, kukui, ironwood, jacaranda, ginger, bamboo. Plenty of times as kids us guys played up there. We knew the place like our own street—the gullies, the stream, the carnation farms. I loved that place.

But now my tongue was so dry it felt twice its size. The sun blasted down through the trees and crawled across my neck. Above, the sky was blue, the clouds clumped somewhere out over the ocean, as far as I could tell. Already Butchie had dark sweat splotches on the back of his shirt.

"What if we see them?" I whispered.

"That's when you take off that safety," Butchie said.

"Then what?"

"What'choo think?"

We hiked single file, crushing the weeds and California grass into a silvery trail. In the sunny spots the earth was warm and soft. All around us, choking vines like giant snakes curled up into the trees. The paratroopers could be anywhere in this place. Maybe they were watching us now, waiting for us to come in the open so they could kill us. My stomach balled up when I thought that, my grip on the Springfield weak with fear.

their homes and businesses at great losses or were forced to

Someone fired. *Bam!*

We hit the ground.

I couldn't tell who shot, only that it wasn't one of us. I dug deep into the knee-high grass. Little black ants crawled on stems and blades inches from my face. I clutched the Springfield close, its oily smell sweet.

"Up front," somebody whispered. "You see anything?"

The point man, who wasn't really a man but a boy like the rest of us, peeked up.

"No. . . . Nothing."

Nobody moved.

When there were no more shots, we slowly got up and crept ahead. I was second to last, Butchie in front of me, and behind me was a white kid, a haole, the last guy. I couldn't go twenty feet without turning around to check if any paratroopers were creeping up behind us. Every time I did that, the haole kid stopped and stared at me, but he never said a word.

"Butchie," I whispered. "What if I have to shoot this rifle? I don't know how. And how can I shoot somebody?"

Butchie stopped and looked back. "Listen to me, Masa. I telling you, you don't shoot them, they going shoot you. You got to shoot, you hear me? You got to."

My shaky hands were gripping the Springfield so tight somebody would have to pry up my fingers with a screwdriver after this day was done. Every part of my body felt electric, like hot jolts racing through my veins. I could have spotted a centipede in the weeds twenty feet away.

abandon them altogether. During the course of the war, ten

A mosquito sang in my ear, and I batted it away.

The stream was close. I couldn't see it, but I could hear the rushing sound. And I could smell it, tangy, like mud and iron. If I could only cup my hands in it and drink... but I had to stay with the platoon.

We crept into a dark, mosquito-infested bamboo grove. Mud squished up between my toes. Sweat beaded down and dripped off my chin. The higher we hiked, the thicker the jungle. Everything was green and brown and steamy.

We moved in silence. The haole kid was grim-faced, keeping his eyes on me like somebody's watchdog every time I looked back. Maybe like me, he was nervous taking up the rear. But it was better than being first.

We broke out of the bamboo into an open space of bushes and grass, two giant monkeypod trees reaching in above us.

I wondered if Mits got the news yet. Probably. And the guys on my team, what were they doing? I guess the game got canceled. Jeez. How can you think about that at a time like—

Ka-pock!

A bullet thwacked into the bamboo grove behind us.

I dropped and bellied into the trail, clutching my rifle in one hand and covering my head with the other. Mud crept into my mouth and seeped into my shirt. Somebody shouted and shot again, and again and again.

Bullets shredded the trees and whirred by above us. Splinters rained down. Leaves evaporated. The bamboo grove cracked apart, a mess of shattered sticks.

people were convicted of spying for Japan—all of whom were

The shooting stopped as suddenly as it had started, the sweet smell of shredded leaves hanging in the air like fresh-cut grass.

Slowly, I peeked up.

Our point man crawled to one of the monkeypod trees and looked around it. He saw something and fired, his rifle jerking. He bolted another round in the chamber and fired again. Four, five, six shots.

A couple of other guys in our group started shooting. At what, I don't know. I couldn't see anything. I fumbled with the safety.

The point man suddenly drew back his rifle. "Wait!" he yelled, motioning for us to stop firing.

Leaning back against the tree, he screamed to whoever was shooting at us. "Cease fire! Cease fire!"

The shooting slowed, one, two shots more.

Then nothing.

Then silence.

"Identify yourself," he yelled into the trees.

Nobody responded.

Then somebody said, "ROTC platoon six...Who are you?"

There was the longest, eeriest silence.

Then our point guy called back. "Platoon four, and if you do that again, I'm going to tear your heart out with my teeth!"

"Sorry."

I never even saw them.

My shirt was really messed up now, mud all over the front and on my arms and face. Butchie looked at me with dark, cave-deep eyes, like he'd just seen the end of his life.

We hiked up the ridge to the top, hiking through the dry pines.

And found nothing.

Not one thing. Not even a footprint.

Nothing but pigs and wild dogs had been up there.

We searched the other side and still found nothing.

Without a word, the lead guy finally signaled for us to head back the way we'd come. Slipping down the steep ridge, I glanced out over the island from spaces where you could see between trees. Pearl Harbor was still burning. But there were still no planes in the sky. Where had they come from, anyway? Had to be a carrier. But how could it have gotten so close?

We hiked back down into the valley and stopped at a grassy bend in the stream. Shady tree branches met in the middle out over the water. Sunlight broke through and sparkled like diamonds in the pools.

"What time is it?" I asked Butchie.

He shrugged.

"Twelve-thirty," the haole guy said. First thing he said all day.

Me and Butchie both looked at him.

I nodded, thanks.

He turned away.

I put my rifle down and knelt and cupped my muddy

hands in the water. I drank deeply. So good, so cool and clean. I lay back in the grass.

"Hey, Butchie," I said, keeping my voice low.

"What?"

"I was going to play baseball today."

Butchie pulled up a weed and studied it.

I slapped at a mosquito.

A moment later, Butchie said, "Kind of a bad day for baseball, Masa."

I laughed. But it wasn't funny.

"Okay, guys, we gotta get moving," our platoon leader said, barely above a whisper.

Nobody complained. We just got up.

"We're going to break up into groups of two and head back down to campus. If there's anyone hiding in this jungle, we'll find 'em."

He started counting off—one two, one two.

"I can't believe they did it," Butchie said, shaking his head.

"No kidding," I said. "They could have killed somebody, shooting like that without even seeing who it was."

"Not them, Masa...Japan."

"Oh."

"What if they land guys on the beaches tonight? What if they come bomb us again?"

I nodded, then shook my head. That thought was worse than worrying about a handful of paratroopers. If they landed on shore, there would be thousands of them. They would swarm all over us.

When he got to me, our platoon leader motioned for me to pair off with the haole.

"But—"

"Let's go," he said, scowling.

Me and the haole headed off.

I glanced back to see where Butchie went, but he was already gone. Everyone was gone, swallowed up by the jungle.

We pushed ahead, me in front and the haole following. It was getting drier now. No more mud, so I knew we were close to campus.

I was thinking about home—about how Mama was doing, and Eldon, and Zip—when the haole finally spoke.

"Hey, Jap," he said.

I stopped and turned around. Jap?

"If we find them ... you gonna shoot them? Or me?"

I gave him a small laugh, thinking this was no time to be joking around like that. But he wasn't joking. His face was like a rock.

We stared at each other.

I couldn't believe it. He really meant it.

I reached out and took the barrel of his Springfield and pointed it right at my chest. "If we find them, who you going shoot? Them or me?"

He didn't blink, thinking what, I don't know.

Then he nodded, once.

With his eyes still on me, he pried my fingers off his rifle.

We moved on.

Jeez.

were race prejudice, war hysteria, and a failure of political

I swatted away the brush with the butt of my Springfield. How could he say that? How could he even think it?

The smoky haze from Pearl Harbor now spread out over the island like a dirty blanket, making everything kind of yellow. Spooky.

Back at the university, we regrouped in silence. If the other guys were like me, their thoughts were all mixed up. And nothing seemed real.

The haole stood near me, waiting for Captain Smith to tell us what to do. Looking away, the haole said, "Sorry for what I said, okay?"

My jaw tightened. I couldn't look at the guy. "Yeah, sure," I said.

He spat, then moved off a couple of steps.

"Are we all here?" Captain Smith said.

No one said we weren't, so Captain Smith told us that President Roosevelt had just declared war on Japan and that the islands were now under martial law. "You all okay? I heard a lot of gunfire."

"We thought we saw something, sir," one guy said.

Captain Smith studied him. "Did you?"

"No sir. It was nothing," the guy added.

Somebody coughed.

Someone else mumbled.

No kidding, I thought. Some of us could be dead.

But we were all still here.

Yeah, still here.

For now.

I'll See You When This War Is Over

M. E. Kerr

I was thirteen the winter everything changed. I knew, even on the cold December night Bud left, that our family would never be the same again. Everyone was at the dinner table: Bud, me, Mom, Dad, my other brother, Tommy, and Hope Hart, from the next town over, Doylestown, Pennsylvania.

No one was saying anything except what began with *Please pass the* ... I hated the way no one would talk about it, but not enough to mention it myself. Someone had left the radio on in the living room. We could hear Radio Dan signing off. He was a Number One cornball, but I listened to him sometimes, secretly. He was the only celebrity I had a personal acquaintance with, never mind he wasn't always sure which Shoemaker kid I was. He lived down at the end of our street. He had this deep, friendly voice. You'd think he'd understand anything you told him. But I knew better. Radio Dan wouldn't understand what Bud was doing, that was for sure.

My father got up, went in, and turned him off. He hardly ever listened to the radio anymore. Everything was about the war.

During World War II, approximately twelve thousand conscientious

A rib roast, Bud's favorite, was being slowly eaten in silence. Even Mahatma, our old collie, who favored Bud over all of us, seemed to sense something dire was taking place. He lay just outside the dining room, his eyes fixed on Bud.

When we finally left the house to take Bud to his train, Mom was crying and hanging on to him. Bud didn't want her to see him off. She said she'd send him some of her gingerbread and macaroons.

"I don't even know if we can get packages from home," Bud said.

"Of course you can!" Mom said.

Dad said, "Maybe he can't. We don't know how they feel about it."

"Well, he's not going to prison, Ef."

"No, he's not, and he's not going to Boy Scout camp, either."

"Ef, what a mean thing to say!"

"I didn't mean it mean."

"Don't send me anything, okay?" Bud said.

Mom cried out, "Come inside, Mahatma! You can't go with him!"

I thought I'd be the one to ride in back with Bud. I couldn't get used to Bud having a steady girl. He'd been with Hope almost two years, but I kept thinking it was like a case of measles or chicken pox — it'd go away in a while.

objectors served in the Civilian Public Service. Another twenty-

"Jubal, ride up here with me and Tom," Dad said.

Tommy put the radio on.

In the back of the Buick, Bud and Hope were sitting so close you'd think there were passengers on either side of them. They were holding hands. Earlier that evening, Hope had given Bud a silver identification bracelet with their initials on the front and "Mind the Light" on the inside.

Hope Hart was a goody two-shoes and an optimist, the kind whose sunny ways wore you down eventually. She had hair a color in between red and brown, and brown eyes. She always knew the right way to walk in and out of rooms, and what to say in them. It was a skill Bud didn't have. He scowled his way through most social gatherings.

Hope was a year older than Bud, and she already had a college degree in home economics. I wanted to like her. I didn't want to blame her for everything that was happening to Bud.

I could hear Hope whispering to Bud, "I love thee. I'll wait for thee, Bud, for as long as need be."

"And I love thee."

They were speaking the old-fashioned "plain language" some Friends still used with family and at Meetings.

Nobody in our family used it until Bud met Hope when he took the summer job on their farm. After that I would hear Bud speak it nights on the telephone. *I think of thee all the time.*

As a young man, Dad did not think of himself as a strict Quaker. He wasn't a regular at the Meeting House. His family way back was, and then he was when he met my mother. Tommy was a lot like Dad used to be. But Bud and I were believers. We would never have considered a school that wasn't Quaker. Bud ultimately chose to go to Swarthmore College. Sometimes when he was home and would speak at Sweet Creek Meeting, I would hear how serious he was about religion. I would be surprised at Bud's anger, telling off Friends there, saying they were some of the most successful businessmen in the county, but did they tithe, did they give 10 percent of their earnings to Friends? Bud bet not! His eyes were fire, and I would be amazed. I also worried that I wasn't as strong as Bud. When it came my time to register for the draft, what kind of a Quaker would I be?

My dad said that it was a good thing Bud had found Hope. Hope, he had said, was more like Bud than Bud was.

"Remember Pearl Harbor," a male chorus sang on the radio.

Dad snapped, "Shut that off!"

"I'll change the station," Tommy said.

"It'll be the same everywhere," Dad grumbled.

Tommy tried, got "Here Comes Santa Claus," tried again and got "White Christmas," tried again and got some news commentator saying the making of automobiles had stopped and the factories were being changed over to airplane and tank factories. In a short time the making of new radios for home use would be cut in half because the materials were needed for the war. Rubber, tin, and aluminum had become

to accept noncombatant roles within the military, and about six precious and were being saved for only the most important uses. Men's suits—

"Turn it off, Tom!"

"Yes sir."

I glanced up at Tommy, and he gave me a weak smile. He was seventeen. Bud was twenty. I was the baby. But all of us looked alike. We all had thick black hair, sturdy builds, and the Shoemaker light blue eyes.

Anyone in Sweet Creek could spot us as Efram Shoemaker's kids. E.F. SHOEMAKER was the sign over the only department store in town. My father called himself E.F. because he'd never liked the name Efram. Most people called him that, anyway. If you never liked the name, why did you give it to Bud? I asked him once. Tradition, the answer came back. There'd been an Efram Shoemaker in Delaware County since the 1600s. Bud was Efram Elam Shoemaker. "Elam" after our grandfather, just as I was Jubal after our great-great-grandfather. Lucky for Tommy that our great-grandfather was named Thomas.

While my father parked the car, Tommy, Hope, Bud, and I went into the station.

When everyone sat down, I asked Bud, "Aren't you going to get a ticket?"

"I already have a ticket, Jube."

"When did you get it?"

"The government's paying his way," Tommy said.

thousand conscientious objectors spent time in prison. Of the

"They are?" I was surprised. I thought that was the last thing the government would do: spring for a ticket for a conscientious objector.

"How long do you have to wait in New York before your train to Colorado?" Hope said. She was wearing her long hair pageboy style. She was in a red plaid pleated skirt with boots and a white turtleneck sweater under a navy blue pea jacket.

"It's just a few hours' wait," Bud said.

"But what will you do at this time of night?" Hope asked.

Bud tried a grin but didn't quite manage it. "There's always something to do in New York," he said, making it sound as though he knew all there was to know about Manhattan. He'd only been there once, years ago, for a Boy Scout jamboree.

Tommy said, "You could call Aunt Lizzy."

"I don't think she'd want me to call her," Bud said.

"Sure she would. You were always her favorite."

"Was," said Bud. "Now, who knows?"

Dad came in from the parking lot, and right behind him was Radio Dan and his kid.

If you didn't know Dan Daniel, you'd never expect that big, deep voice.

In person, Radio Dan was plump and medium-height, balding, with a beer belly. He always wore polka-dot bow ties, blue ones, green ones, yellow ones. Were they clip-ons? He

men drafted during World War II, only about one-tenth of one liked to wear V-neck sleeveless sweaters, the same color, with them.

"Shhhoot!" Tommy said. "Radio Dan and Dean!"

"So act like who cares," I said.

"Who does care?" Bud shrugged.

Everyone seemed to be saying good-bye at railroad or bus stations those days. There were uniforms everywhere. Some of the guys wearing them looked to me like kids dressed up to play war games in their backyards.

That's what Dean Daniel looked like that evening—this skinny boy dressed up like a marine. His ears stuck out at the sides of his cap. He'd been my junior counselor in Cub Scout camp one summer, but he'd called for his folks to come and get him because he was terrified of spiders. Dean was a twin, but when you saw him with Danny Jr., they didn't even look like brothers. Danny Jr. looked tough, and he was.

The Daniels waved at us and sat down on a bench nearby. Radio Dan was lighting a cigarette and passing the pack to Dean.

My father's ears were red. I'd always thought he wasn't comfortable with what Bud was doing. He'd never said as much, but I had overheard conversations between Mom and him, and I'd heard him say he wasn't sure he would have made the same decision.

"Is the train on time?" Dad asked Tommy. His voice was so low, Tommy had to ask him what he said.

He said it again, then shuffled his feet and stole a glance back at the Daniels.

Everyone in Sweet Creek knew about Bud, particularly Radio Dan. He knew all the town gossip. Nothing was secret for long in a town of twenty thousand. Bud had been asked not to lead his Boy Scout troop last fall. When he drove up at Texaco in his old Ford with the "A" gas-rationing sticker on the windshield, the help took their time coming out to collect his coupon and gas him up. It was the same when he stopped at Sweet Creek Diner for coffee, or went into Acme Food Stores for groceries. No one wanted to be of service to Bud Shoemaker.

"Please don't wait for the train," Bud said.

"We want to wait with you, Bud," Dad said.

"We're waiting," said Tommy.

"I don't want you to wait," Bud said.

I sang a little of "Wait 'Til the Sun Shines, Nellie," trying to provide some comic relief. But I knew there was no such thing as relief for Bud's situation. It was just going to get worse every day the war lasted.

I went into the Men's, and Tommy followed me.

"I bet Dad hates having Radio Dan here!" Tommy said.

I knew that Tommy hated it, too. Dean was home on leave from boot camp in Parris Island, South Carolina. His twin had joined the marines when he was seventeen.

A few days ago, Tommy and I had run into Dean in town in front of the bank. He was with his kid sister, Darie, her hair soft and tawny. She was my age but older-looking and

-acting, the way girls have of becoming people before boys do. She didn't bother to greet me, just stood there regarding me with these cool, bored eyes, as though in her short time on this planet she had rarely been subjected to an encounter with anyone as ordinary as I was.

Dean punched his palm with his fist and told us he couldn't wait to kill a Jap. Then he covered his mouth with his hand and said, "Whoops! Wrong guy to tell that to!"

Tommy shrugged and said, "I'm not partial to Japs."

"You'd never kill one, I bet!" Darie Daniel piped up. She was always in Sweet Creek High plays, particularly ones with music. Twice a night there was a recording of her singing Radio Dan's theme song. I'd seen her in a few Gilbert and Sullivan operettas. She was cocky, a little tomboyish, and she could belt a song so you'd hear it down to City Hall.

Folks went past us, in and out of the bank. Tommy answered, "I doubt I'd ever kill anyone."

"Even if someone was holding a gun to your mother's head?" Darie Daniel said. "What would you do then?"

"I'd sic my bulldog here on him." Tommy ruffled my hair and grinned down at me.

Bud had told us the draft board asked him those kind of questions. *What would you do if you saw a man raping a woman? What if foreign invaders came on your street; would you help fight them?*

"Let's drop the subject," Dean said. "It's the last thing I want to talk about when I'm home on leave."

"I know how to shoot a gun," Darie Daniel said. "And I'd

have no compunction about blasting away if anyone dared hurt a member of my family!"

That night while he washed his hands beside me in the Men's, Tommy muttered, "Radio Dan's going to mention this, wait and see!"

"Probably," I agreed.

"At least Darie wasn't with them," Tommy said.

"Who cares about Darie?"

"I go to the same school with her! You don't!"

"It's Bud I feel sorry for," I said. "Did you notice Radio Dan said all our names but his?"

When we came back out, Tommy checked on Bud's train and called out, "Track three. All aboard, Bud!"

The Daniels got up, too. There was only one train heading for Manhattan.

Suddenly, servicemen seemed to come from everywhere, all heading for track three.

Dad stopped and held up his hand. "We'll say our good-byes here."

He hugged Bud and then Tommy did.

"I'll miss you, Bud," I said.

Bud bent down and held me tight. "I'll see you when this war is over. You take care of Mom," he said.

"Okay, I will."

"I'll write you from Colorado," Bud told us.

Radio Dan and his boy had stopped a few feet away.

1972, when more draftees were granted exemptions than were

"Take care of yourself, son!" that fabulous voice rang out.

After our good-byes, we left Hope standing alone with Bud, locked in this long kiss, and headed for the exit.

Radio Dan was also headed toward the only exit there was.

Because Bud was a conscientious objector, he was going to a Civilian Public Service Camp. But I was still in the dark about what would become of him next. I had the feeling he didn't know himself.

Last fall, he'd received a list of things he should pack. There was everything there from "two pairs of medium-weight long underwear with long sleeves and legs" to "three bed sheets good quality, at least 63 by 99 inches."

Radio Dan paused to light another cigarette.

"What's going to happen to Bud now?" I asked my father, keeping my voice down. "Will he have a job?"

"Wait until we get home."

E. F. Shoemaker Company and radio station WBEA were on the same side of Pilgrim Lane, a few doors from each other. Tuesdays Dad and Radio Dan went to Rotary together. Before Rotary, Dad would stop by the radio station to pick up Radio Dan and walk down to Sweet Creek Inn with him for the luncheon meeting.

And there the two of them were at the train station: one seeing his second son off to war, and Dad seeing Bud off to Colorado, about as far away from any war as he could get.

When Hope caught up with us, for the first time her eyes had a watery look, but she was holding her chin up, smiling.

inducted into the armed services. (4)

She said, "Bud's going to be fine!" Then, probably for Radio Dan's benefit, "I'm so proud of him!"

"Well, we all are, we all are," Dad said in a voice so low we could hardly hear it.

The four of us walked silently to the car, not talking, until Tommy suddenly blurted out, "This damn, damn war!"

Golpe de Estado

Dian Curtis Regan

The lives of all of us are stories.
If enough of these stories are told,
then perhaps we will begin to see
that our lives are the same story.
The differences are merely in the details.
—Julius Lester

February 4, 1992
Low-flying planes startle me awake.

Squeezing my eyes, I try to capture my interrupted dream before it puffs off into darkness and is forgotten. I was dreaming of Denver. Hanging with Stray and Camp. Don't ask how they got the nicknames. I wasn't Zack with them; I was Whip. I miss being Whip.

Another plane shreds the predawn sky, followed by rumblings. Thunder? In the dry season? I've been in Caracas only three weeks—not long enough to know what is normal and what is not. I decide to ignore it as I fumble for the light on my watch. Five-fifteen. Almost time to get up for another day of faking like I know what people are saying.

I think about homeroom at CIV—Colegio Internacional de Venezuela. Eight students. Three embassy kids— American, Chinese, and Brazilian. Another oil-patch kid, like me, and three very wealthy Venezuelans (I have labeled them VWVs.)

I have nothing in common with any of them, except perhaps Armando (a VWV), who lives here in the Dorado Apartments and speaks English better than most. He promised to teach me "important" Spanish words so I'll have *asfalto*— street smarts.

First lesson was the F-word. Except here, it's the C-word and sounds as harmless as a kitten's name. (Imagine: Fluffy you!)

The American embassy guy, Doug, is obnoxious. He riffs every morning on the ills of Venezuela. As a fellow American, this embarrasses me. A guest shouldn't criticize the host to his face. I mean, yeah, Mom gets going on what's wrong with traffic-glutted, crime-ridden Caracas, but she'd never rag in front of our driver, Humberto, or any other *Caraqueño*. I figure the VWVs hate the ugly American.

Before I can doze off, someone bangs on the front door. I listen, wondering if I should answer it. My dad gave *strict orders* never to open the door unless I'm expecting someone. This command is always followed by stories of kidnapped ex-pat kids held for ransom. And maimed or tortured or killed.

I wait, wondering if Dad, who dumped us here in the big city and went off to work in Punto Fijo, wanted to scare me into a state of paranoid caution. Whatever. It worked.

wo years in prison for attempting to overthrow the government,

Voices tell me Mom has let someone in.

Curious, I get up and pull on a pair of cargo shorts *sin* shirt and shoes. In the living room, I find Armando from 3B, dressed the same way.

"*¿Qué pasa?*" I ask. What's happening?

In answer, he clicks on the TV and switches to Venevisión, a local station. I see Perez, the president, yelling into a microphone. The camera cuts to a shot of Miraflores, the presidential palace. Tanks are ramming the gates.

Mom curses, her patience already rubbed thin by an air-conditioner repairman who never showed and a plumber who came four hours late, then walked off with her tools.

Hey, we were warned that Venezuelans live on elastic time, but for my efficient American mother and her DayPlanner, this is torture.

I stare at the TV. A news camera jiggles as the crew runs. Gunfire pops as they skirt a burning car.

Watching the scene play out only blocks from our apartment shakes my American sensibility. Feeling rubbery, I sink to the couch, hoping no one notices how it's affected me. Jeesh, I just figured out how to order a McDonald's *hamburguesa,* and now I have to deal with this?

Mom forcefully clicks off the television, as if that will stop the attack. "Armando, how did you know this was happening?"

"CIV phone tree. Señor Blanco call one student. He call the next, and on down the line until the last student call back to the teacher."

even launching a second failed coup from prison in November 1992

Mom's face is a mixture of fear and betrayal—certainly aimed at Malcolm Oil, who sent us here. "Does stuff like this happen a lot?"

Armando shrugs. "Workers strike. Students of the university burn tires in the streets. Floods bring looters. The phone tree is the only way to tell everyone school is cancel."

"Wait," I say. "What exactly is happening?" I'd watched political chaos on TV a million times, but it's always halfway around the world. Today *I'm* halfway around the world, and it's happening in my face.

I yank back the drapes. In the dark, it looks as if a fireworks display is exploding way too close to the ground. The sight chills me in spite of the tropical humidity.

"A lieutenant colonel in the army of Perez tries to throw over the government," Armando explains. "His name Chávez."

"Oh, lord," Mom mumbles. "We move here and they stage a coup."

"*Un golpe de estado,*" Armando adds, as if saying it in Spanish clarifies the situation.

"So, what are we supposed to do?" I peek outside again, willing daylight to hurry so I can see what's going on. In spite of the fear, a sense of excitement races through my veins.

Armando's eyes are taking stock of our apartment. I wonder what he is thinking. "They order—stay inside until more we know." He backs toward the door. "I go to call the next person for you. Hey, Zack, come down later."

"Sure," I say, trying to sound casual. It's the first time

n 1998, vowing to end corruption, he was elected president of anyone has included me in plans. Okay, they're not really plans, but still, I'm pleased.

"You're not going anywhere," Mom says as soon as the door shuts.

It surprises me. I figure she wants me to make friends. "I'm not going to Miraflores, Mom, just to the third floor." I look at her with an unexpected rush of male protectiveness and notice gray in her hair. Had it been there before the move? I don't remember.

She grasps my arm. "This could be serious, Zack. The company might want to get us out. We need to stay together."

Wow. The hope of Malcolm Oil sending a jet to rescue us brightens my morning. I hurry to dress so I'm ready in case we have to bravely fight our way to the roof to catch a U.S. helicopter.

Noon

So much for a "here comes the cavalry" rescue.

I sprawl on the couch, bored, dying of the heat, likewise cursing the A/C guy *plus* the delinquent phone installer— not that I have anyone to call.

I think of a girl at CIV—Ana Bello from Argentina. Eyes as black as the frigate birds riding the thermals, buzzing our twelfth-floor windows. Hair that melts around her shoulders. I secretly believe if I could touch her hair, I would sail through the semester unscathed—filled with confidence, fluent in *español*.

Venezuela in a landslide victory. After rewriting the constitution to

Suddenly my grandparents barge into my fantasy without even knocking. Ana's image politely scurries away. I'll bet Gram and Grandad will be worried sick about us when the news hits the *Denver Post*. Or is a South American civil war important enough to warrant more than a paragraph on an inside page?

Guilt shoves me off the couch. How many times have I skipped uninterested over headlines such as FIGHTING ERUPTS IN BOTSWANA?

Ugly American indeed.

Sudden activity on TV catches my eye. Two planes begin a dogfight in the sky. Awesome! I grapple for the remote to turn on the sound I'd muted earlier after the rapid-fire Spanish started getting on my nerves.

Before I can raise the volume, a roar pains my ears. I run to the window. The same two planes dip and bank in a deadly dance as they try to blow each other out of the sky. I can see the fight on TV *and* from the living room window at the same time. Amazing! Wait till I tell Camp and Stray!

"Zack, get away from the windows!"

Mom closes the drapes and shoos me into the kitchen, where I can't even watch the fight on television. Her argument about raining bullets is a good one, though, and before I can complain, the electricity cuts off, silencing the TV. Outside, whining engines rip the air, then slam to a stop with a cryptic abruptness. It *kills* me not to know what happened.

extend his term from five to a possible twelve years, he staged

Mom gives up trying to call Dad on the cell phone Malcolm Oil provided for emergencies. She fixes cheese on crackers. I hate seeing her hands shake in apprehension as she works.

We don't have much food because she hasn't figured out shopping yet. Humberto explained how one goes to a *panadería* for bread, a *carnicería* for meat, and a *frutería* for vegetables. Mom has no intention of spending an entire day in Caracas *tráfico* just to shop. She believes she and her DayPlanner can organize Venezuela. Clean it up and fix it. Send all the bad guys to their rooms. I say it's a good sign she's thinking like a North American.

Seven P.M.

Mom finds a box of macaroni and cheese, but it's useless without electricity. We scavenge some dead bread and make (untoasted) cheese sandwiches, eating in the glow of one candle and two flashlights. Afterward, she fixes me a bowl of Tío Rico cho-co-LAH-te ice cream, afraid it will melt all over the freezer. She buys it but won't eat it. Her usual fat-free frozen yogurt is not to be found in a Third World country where hunger is a greater concern than weight loss.

Outside, it's grown quiet except for occasional gunfire. I pretend I'm hearing pop-bottle rockets instead of bullets; it takes the edge off my anxiety.

*   *   *

another election in 2000 to put the new constitution into effect. His

Nine P.M.

Feeling an unspoken need to stay in the same room, Mom and I play cards by candlelight. I've just fixed a second bowl of ice cream when, up from the streets, a low clanking begins. Mom and I look at each other. In the soft candlelight her face appears young, her eyes tinged with dread. I know she is worried about Dad. She finally got through to him. He's stuck in Punto Fijo, trying to get a *salvo conducto* permit from the *Guardia Nacional* to allow him safe passage to Caracas.

The faraway clanking grows louder. And nearer. The creepy noise draws me to the window in spite of Mom's protests. What's going on? This is freakin' unnerving.

I see people swarming into the streets, banging pots and pans. In the moonlight, outlines are blurred, creating a ghostly effect. They ooze across the avenue, surrounding the Dorado. A sea of angry people, powerless, yet wanting their presence to be known.

The mass clanking becomes deafening, nerve rattling, terror inducing. Totally spooked, I stumble back to the kitchen in the dark to make sure Mom is okay. She is so shaken, she is eating my ice cream.

I check the door to make sure it's locked.

I check the door again.

And again.

February 5

The rising sun hunches behind slow-moving clouds, as if

main opponent, Francisco Arias Cárdenas, a former brother-in-arms hiding, as it makes its way above a troubled city. The streets are unearthly quiet.

From my room, I gaze out the window at the alien view. To the north, I'm surprised to see skyscrapers still standing after last night. They make Caracas look like any major city, yet mask the poverty surrounding downtown. The flashy SIEMPRE COCA-COLA sign towers over the freeway, implying, "We are all the same. We all drink Coke." To the south, row after row of dirty concrete-block houses bake in the heat. For those who can afford them, metal bars take the place of windows, and papaya trees grow in enclosed yards. But most of the huts have dirt floors and broken chairs out front, where families sit in the street at night, searching for cooler air.

From my window, I see a girl, maybe ten years old, in front of her graffitied wall. She's there every day, selling *queso de mano* or *tortas*. While she waits for customers, she plays ball with a stick and a rock. Today, no one is on the street. The girl sits in her gateway, looking stunned. When this is over, I will buy *tortas* from her.

Across rooftops, Mt. Avila's lumpy spine juts above the city like a prehistoric dragon. It makes me think of the Colorado mountains. Surely, Denver is a deep freeze on this February morning, yet here I am staring at palm trees—which would be cool if I were on vacation, but I am not. The phrase "It's a nice place to visit, but I wouldn't want to live there" teases my mind and makes me shake my head.

This morning, I am thankful to have water for a shower

and electricity for coffee. I eat the last boiled egg and the last slice of bread. Then I read, catch up on homework, pace, watch TV, play Nintendo, and pace. Sometime after three, the power goes out again. I cannot stand to stay in this apartment a moment longer.

Mom is on a cell-phone rampage after finding out that teachers at CIV knew danger was brewing early enough to stock up on food and water—but did not warn the parents.

I am glad she is on the phone so I don't have to argue with her. I jot a note so she will know where I went, then slip out.

On the third floor, I tap on Armando's door. His mother, Señora Cordero, appears.

"Bienvenido," she says. *"Adelante."*

Armando swoops me into his room. Doug-the-obnoxious is lounging at the computer desk. My stomach clenches when I see him, but I say, "Hey," and try not to act surprised that he and Armando are friends.

Doug's family lives down the boulevard in a *quinta,* a house with a live-in maid, a gardener, a pool, and a satellite dish capable of picking up U.S. TV stations. He fills me in on CNN news:

The coup attempt failed. Chávez has been arrested. However, *la gente,* the people, are still riled up in favor of the revolutionaries. Snipers are shooting at buildings and at people in line for food. Martial law has been declared, including a curfew from six P.M. until six A.M. Schools are canceled for the rest of the week.

And worse. Doug tells us that a senior at CIV was shot

straying from their original revolutionary ideals. Arias claimed and killed in the doorway of her house by stray gunfire. Paola Vargas. I fake a sudden interest in Armando's CD collection so they don't see how much this rattles me. Paola had this incredible giggle and always said *"Hola."* I feel like crying, even though I didn't really know her.

Armando's mother comes to the door with *arepas*. We dive in, scarfing down the cornmeal patties. I'd gotten into the habit of stopping at Rosa's *Panadería* on the way to school to buy *arepas*. On the way home, I'd grab an *empanada* and *Chinotto* to drink.

My mom doesn't "get" *arepas* or *empanadas*. She thinks they are grease city.

Armando and his mom chatter in Spanish. After a language crash course on audiotapes I got for Christmas, I can pick out words, but not content.

I hear *"comida"* and hope we're being invited to dinner. Mom is running out of cheese and crackers and doesn't have the old standby, peanut butter, because she can't find it. Venezuelans don't "get" peanut butter. Ha.

Armando faces us. "You want to look for food?"

Doug immediately springs to his feet. "Sure, let's go."

I hesitate. Besides the fact that it's less than two hours until curfew and I've left the apartment without permission, I recall the news about snipers.

Señora Cordero returns and hands Armando a stack of *bolivares*. She tells us in broken English to be quick and cautious. Armando shoves the money into his pocket. *"¿Listo?"* he asks. "Ready?"

Chávez had turned a blind eye to corruption and was running a sham

Doug notes my hesitancy and sneers. "Gotta ask your mommy first?"

Testosterone pumps my muscles. I look away to avoid smashing his face. *Yeah, Whip, he's right, but you'd never admit it.* "Let's hurry," I say, tapping my watch to imply we haven't got much time. I'll deal with Mom later. Maybe if I return with food, she won't report my blatant misbehavior to Dad.

We leave the Dorado Apartments. Streets are deserted. Not one rusty, falling-apart '77 Chevy in sight. We walk down a garbage-strewn *calle*, stepping over potholes. Rosa's *Panadería* is dark and empty—closed like every other shop. Where are we supposed to buy food?

A pack of mangy dogs makes us hurry our steps. Stray dogs and cats line the gutters like litter, useless and ignored. This kills my mother, who wants to feed them all, but we were warned at our Malcolm Oil security briefing not to touch street animals.

A distant *tat-tat-tat* stops us. I begin to sweat. The machine-gun fire is blocks away, but it's coming from the direction we're heading. We turn down a different street.

Before my heart can stop pounding, three F-16 fighter jets scream across the sky, followed by more gunshots.

"American-built," Doug snips. His conceit streaks across the sky with the jet trail. "So," he continues, "if the revolutionaries were doing this to save the people from a corrupt government, how can they justify killing innocent people who got in the way?"

Armando leaves the question dangling in the air. I think

democracy while concentrating power in his own hands. Regardless, of Paola and wonder how many others have died. Who exactly is the enemy? The corrupt government? Or a dissatisfied lieutenant slaughtering civilians?

Who do we trust? The president, assuring TV viewers everything is okay? Or Chávez, dressed as a typical revolutionary in his battle fatigues and red beret, as though he's watched too many war movies? He urges the masses to fight for their rights. *El soberano*, he calls them. The sovereign.

I want to believe in Chávez's dream, but he is in jail right now.

Six blocks from the apartments, we find an open *mercado*. People are jammed inside. Shelves are almost empty. Armando grabs cans of Comuna peaches and Los Andes shelf milk. There's no bread or fresh anything. Not one carton of Tio Rico for my mom not to eat. The electricity is out, and the smell of rotting fish is sickening.

I move through the crowd toward the cashiers, picking up candy, crackers, cheese, and a can of tuna. I don't know how many *bolivares* I have, so I'm afraid of taking too much. Twenty-five sweaty minutes later, we have moved through the long lines and paid without working cash registers. There are no bags, so I stuff everything into my cargo shorts, glad for the extra pockets.

By the time we get outside, it's half past five. I can't imagine how much trouble I will be in if I get arrested after curfew. Or worse—get caught in the line of fire. I don't even have my passport, which is mandatory. I wasn't planning on going anywhere.

Chávez easily won reelection. Today he is considered South

"Let's hustle," I say. Doug smirks. I force myself to ignore him.

Sounds of a shouting mob send us on yet another detour. *Avoid noises of any kind,* I think. *Hello, paranoid caution.*

I wish Armando and Doug were Stray and Camp, with our "we can conquer the world" attitude. The way Stray would mouth off and then Camp, all 220 pounds of him, would rise up tall, daring anyone to mess with us. Like a cat puffing its tail. Worked every time.

I'm on a street I don't know. I see a *farmacia* and note it for later since Mom was needing Tylenol. I'm about to ask Armando if there is any such thing as Tylenol in Venezuela when five guys loom menacingly ahead of us. They are definitely not VWVs.

Armando spits out a Spanish curse I haven't learned yet. Then, "*Ladrones.* Thieves. Keep walking." He leads us to the other side of the street.

Doug is cursing in English. That I understand.

I face the scowling Latinos, certain that my blond hair does not endear me to them. I reach for my apartment key, thinking it's the closest thing I have to a weapon. Or I could pelt the *ladrones* with crackers and candy. Toss cheese into their eyes. My brain is whirling with plans of defense, but my shaking knees do not get the message.

As my dad says, "The have-nots strike out against the haves no matter what society you're in." We are the haves. They are the have-nots.

America's most colorful and unpredictable leader and meets often

Suddenly, the group is barreling toward us, shouting words I don't know yet understand completely.

"Run!" Doug hollers.

I'm glad he's the one who yells it and not me.

I cut down a side street seconds before I realize that three against five might not be bad odds. Armando is no Camp, but he's big. I wouldn't want to mess with him.

Too late.

Two sets of footsteps pound after me with the same *tat-tat* rhythm of the machine guns, now popping erratically nearby. I am running toward the hot spot instead of home.

Brilliant, Whip.

For someone used to living a mile above sea level in a cold climate, I'm having a tough time huffing air so thick, it enters my lungs and stays.

Ahead of me, an army tank rolls across the intersection. A massive, rumbling reminder that I'm caught in the middle of somebody else's war.

I falter.

A hand grabs the back of my shirt. Twisting, I swing blindly. Dodging my fist, the guy jabber-shouts at me. I can't respond because all my Spanish flies out of my head. I figure he is demanding *dinero*. I'm still clutching my key-weapon, but if all they want is money and not my life, then fine. Take it.

I dig into my pocket and pull out the remaining *bolivares*.

The boy removes the bills from my hand and the watch from my wrist in one swift movement. I am too impressed to mourn the loss of my Casio.

with the person he calls his mentor: Cuba's Communist dictator,

I meet his gaze, suddenly realizing he's just a kid. Twelve, maybe, but tall enough to make you think he's older. His accomplice is even younger.

"*Vete!*" the boy growls, trying to scare me away.

I am weak with relief to know they are finished with me. But I do not run. I stare at the torn, filthy clothes, the patched shoes. Rage boils inside me. Not at these kids, but at the second-richest oil country in the world. How dare they allow so many of their people to live in *ranchitos* and *barrios?*

Forgetting any *asfalto* I might have acquired, I blurt, "Wait."

They react like cats, poised to flee, yet curious. At that instant, I realize they are as afraid of me as I am of them.

I reach into the deep pockets of the cargo shorts and pull out my piddly stash of snacks. They creep close, as if thinking it's a trap. I stand still, holding out the loot. They snatch it and fade into the dusky night so fast, I think I imagined it.

Tat-tat-tat.

I flinch at the shots, suddenly terrified to be alone on the street at twilight. I run, stopping at corners, scanning the sky-line until I spot the Dorado. Don't know if it's after curfew since I no longer own a watch.

The electricity is back on, so I take the elevator to the third floor. Armando opens the door. A fresh cut oozes across his cheek, making me wince.

"You okay?" he asks.

"Me? Yeah. Are *you* okay?"

Fidel Castro. Meanwhile, Venezuela remains oil-rich yet poverty-

"Besides this"—he pauses to touch his cheek—"I am more poor, but alive. I save the food, but not Doug."

My heart skitters. "You what?"

"I warn Doug not to mouth off, but he does. They was hard on him. He is more poor now, like me, only he find his way home in his underwear."

I crack up, even though it must have been awful. Armando laughs with me and instantly the joke bonds us. I will enjoy a semester of hanging with him. The fact that he is friends with Ana Bello certainly won't hurt.

I head for the twelfth floor, grateful not to be showing up with a knife slash but sorry to be empty-handed—not to mention out an entire week's allowance. As I suspected, Mom is hyperventilating and ready to murder me. I give her a safe "mother version" of the story. What can she do? Ground me? I'm already grounded. So is she.

The doorbell rings, and we both tense until we recognize the voice. It's Humberto, arriving with groceries five minutes before curfew.

When a mother is starving, a gift of soup and chicken makes her forget about murdering her only son. Thank you, Humberto.

We dine well. Humberto stays to regale us with stories (in Spanglish) of the '88 Caracas riots, which have culminated in the present coup. It's a case of history repeating itself. Those in power pocket a country's wealth while the masses suffer—until someone comes along to upset the stranglehold.

Against our protests, Humberto defies the curfew and

stricken. Chávez still wears battle fatigues with a red beret, and he slips out into the darkness, assuring us that he knows all the back streets and alleys to his home.

I head for my room to unclench my still tense muscles. Suddenly, I feel the need to check on the little girl across the street, making sure she's tucked in safely for the night. The street is empty. Cursing the broken A/C, I slide open a window, not caring about mosquitoes. Immediately I feel guilty. At least I *have* air-conditioning—or will as soon as it's repaired.

Glancing around my room, I see other things I have: a computer, TV, Nintendo. I am one of the haves.

I gaze up at Mt. Avila's twinkling *barrios*. At night, the dragon mountain and its hoarded jewels are incredibly beautiful. At dawn, the ugliness returns.

Dad says lights in the *barrios* means stolen electricity. So what? Let the poor steal light and heat—something we take for granted until we don't have it.

I wonder if the *ladrones* live on the mountain. I wonder if their lives would have gotten better if the coup had succeeded. Or would Chávez simply have become another Perez?

I wonder if the boys' families are dining on crackers and cheese tonight—like Mom and I did yesterday. *Man,* I think, *maybe we are way more alike than different.*

Stepping into my closet, I grab the baseball Stray and I used to toss around at Cherry Creek Park. In a bag, I find the bat Dad gave me for my fifteenth birthday. It's a good one, an aluminum H&B.

I have to steal through the empty maid's quarters to get

has turned the anniversary of the coup attempt into a national day out the door without Mom hearing me. I go down the elevator and across the street as silently as a *ladrone*. I creep along the graffitied wall until I come to the right gate. Reaching between the bars, I toss the ball and bat along the inside wall.

She'll find them in the morning.

Snap, Crackle, Pop

Lois Metzger

Most people "fell" in love. But when it came to Grace Hamilton, Ben Forster felt as though he were spinning through space, warmed by the sun..."tumble-toasted," as it said on the cereal box.

Snap! Crackle! Pop! Kellogg's Rice Krispies never say anything more. But they never say anything less. That's because they're Tumble-Toasted by an exclusive process that spins them full of crispy goodness and makes them golden toasty all over!

Ben lifted the bowl to his lips to get the last of the cereal, which had become soggy and wasn't saying much at this point.

"Oh, Benny." His mother, wearing a light coat and a hat, stood in the kitchen doorway. She always sounded mournful when he did things like that. Drank from the bowl. Wiped his mouth on his sleeve.

"Mom, nobody's here to see me."

"*I'm* here!"

"Yeah, but you don't count."

"Thanks a heap!"

They had this conversation, or something like it, nearly every morning. She always knew he was kidding, and she

"On May 15, 1954, in the high summer of the great fear, the

always pretended to be offended. She was his mom, his predictable, dependable, cheerful mom—his only parent since his father died nearly eight years before, in 1946. Benny loved her very much. He just didn't want to think about her.

He preferred to fill his thoughts with Grace Hamilton... with her long yellow hair swept up in a ponytail that bounced when she walked. Grace's hair was always sparkly, like she shampooed it between classes or something. She had big dark eyes and peachy skin and a clear, lilting voice that got her the lead in all the school musicals. She also had a figure like Marilyn Monroe's.

Ben was exactly her age, fourteen, a ninth grader, but Grace considered fourteen-year-old, ninth-grade boys little better than infants. She dated college men (or so Ben had heard). Still, Ben knew that he and Grace were meant for each other. He joined the chorus, just to be near her two afternoons a week. They both had Mrs. Dinsby for social studies, seventh period. Sometime and somewhere, Grace had to notice him.

But she was so busy! Besides the chorus and the musicals, she was a pom-pom girl, and the head of the D.D.A.R.—the Daughters of the Daughters of the American Revolution— and she was always surrounded by dozens of best friends (Ben only had one best friend, and he'd moved away over Christmas break). Grace's mother was something of a big deal, too, a former national golf champion, a regional beauty pageant winner, a direct descendant of a *Mayflower* family, and now head of the Silver Falls High School PTA. She came

to school a lot for meetings and to drop Grace off in a dark
green convertible. Mrs. Hamilton always wore a fluttery scarf
around her throat. You could tell that she had been quite
beautiful—in her time. But this, May 1954, was Grace's time.

"Benny—" His mother wasn't saying her usual morning
good-bye. He noticed she was holding the newspaper, the
Pittsburgh Post-Gazette. Ben preferred to read cereal boxes. "I,
um, there's something I think we should..." She paused.

Ben looked at her curiously.

"Oh, never mind!" She smiled brightly. "I love you, see
you at dinner, I'll make tuna casserole with onion rings!"

That was more like her usual morning good-bye, onion
rings and all.

Several years ago, Ben and his mother had moved to Silver
Falls, Pennsylvania, from Riverton, Illinois—a place practi-
cally halfway across the country—because it was safe.
Because the people were friendly. You couldn't walk down a
street in Silver Falls without somebody saying hello, and
smiling, and asking how you were and waiting for the answer.
Riverton, his mother had said, was not a safe, friendly place.
Here, there were good schools and a good library (where
Ben's mother was now the head librarian), and it was beautiful, besides. Green paths led to gentle hills, and there were
lakes to skate on and swim in, and there was Silver Falls
itself, which got its name because it looked silver in fading
light. "Young people love the falls!" his mother said. "They

civil liberties in the United States today is the most serious in drive from all over just to see it!" Ben found out from his best friend just what they did in their cars when they weren't looking at the falls.

Best of all, Ben was happy here. His mother was happy here, too. She woke up singing.

Maybe not that particular morning, he realized. And wondered about that.

When Ben got to social studies, Mrs. Dinsby was holding up that week's issue of *Life* magazine. "Students, this is deadly serious," she began. "Deadly, deadly serious."

Ben knew what was coming. Whenever Mrs. Dinsby said something was "deadly serious" or "frightfully important" or "in dire need of our utmost attention," she would talk about the atomic bomb that Russia was going to drop on us. Sometimes, in the middle of a lesson, Mrs. Dinsby would call out, "Duck and cover!" and everyone would have to put their hands over their heads and squat under their wooden desks.

Some kids took this seriously. Some made fun of it, yawning or laughing. For Ben, this war—the Cold War, it was called—was merely a romantic backdrop to his life with Grace. When the bomb fell, he could protect her, give her his desk, as well as her own, to hide beneath. They could run to a bomb shelter—there was one only three blocks away, with a black-and-yellow triangle inside a circle to let you know it was there. He would make sure she had a blanket. If they couldn't reach a shelter in time, he would take her to his

the history of our country.' It was indeed a desperate time, house, which had a basement. She had one of those newer, split-level homes that only had a garage.

"There's a wonderful article—well, I can't say wonderful, because it's so deadly serious. Let's call it a helpful, well-done article. It's all about how to evacuate our major cities when the Communist bombs start falling. Look at this." Mrs. Dinsby held up a photograph of Washington, D.C. "This is Ground Zero," she said, and pointed to the center. Sure enough, it was labeled GROUND ZERO. There was a huge circle around Ground Zero, with the words TOTAL DESTRUCTION. Another, wider circle farther out was labeled MODERATE DAMAGE.

"These arrows indicate the roads where people can walk to safety," she explained. "This is where car pools will have to go."

Ben could car-pool Grace to safety! Once he got his license.

"Mrs. Dinsby?" A girl named Cindy raised her hand.

"Yes, Miss Dale?"

"Mrs. Dinsby, isn't that other picture a picture of Pittsburgh?"

Mrs. Dinsby sighed. "Yes. The article has demonstrated the damage that will be done to Pittsburgh, St. Louis, San Francisco, and Spokane."

Ben had heard that some kids, fear-struck about the bomb, couldn't sleep. No doubt Cindy was one of these, her voice was so tiny and shaky. "But Silver Falls is so close to Pittsburgh. Doesn't it fall in the 'total destruction' circle?"

"Yes, I believe it does." Mrs. Dinsby patted her tall orange hair, fluffy and stiff as cotton candy. "So far, I regret to say, Pittsburgh has no evacuation plan for its million citizens, not to mention those of us in the nearby suburbs." She squinted at the article. "San Francisco has a plan. It's a particularly vulnerable city because it is surrounded by water, but citizens can escape on foot over two bridges and four highways...."

Ben imagined sirens splitting the night, running with Grace, the bomb falling, the bright, fat mushroom cloud behind them. Strange, this Cold War that wasn't really a war. Not a Hot War, or at least not yet, with real explosions and injuries and deaths. But we hate the Russians and they hate us, Mrs. Dinsby had explained. So we point bombs at them and they point bombs at us.

Who would kill first, America or Russia? Who would die first?

"Mrs. Dinsby."

Ben looked up, suddenly alert.

That was Grace, who never bothered to raise her hand, and whose voice, unlike Cindy's, was loud and confident. "If we knew there were Communists in our community, wouldn't you say that, as true Americans, we ought to expose them?"

"Absolutely," Mrs. Dinsby responded without hesitation.

That was the other side to this war. The enemy, "them," was Communist Russia, that blotlike country halfway across the world that took up so much of the map. But there were also enemies hidden among "us." Communists, here in

America. You couldn't tell by looking at them, or listening to them, if they were, in fact, Communists; they led secret, underground lives. But there were stories in the newspapers about Communists trying to infiltrate America, one town at a time.

Ben wasn't exactly sure how this would work—when the bombs fell, wouldn't they land on some of their own, too?

Grace stood, to give herself room to talk. She had on a string of pearls and a lilac sweater that was thrillingly too tight for her. "I mean, let's say someone worked with children— a teacher, maybe. And she was a Communist. And she was trying to take over a place like Silver Falls. Through the children, influencing young minds! We have a patriotic duty, don't we, to expose her, even if that means she loses her job or goes to jail, even?"

Mrs. Dinsby, suddenly pale, stared at Grace. A teacher? Who worked with children? In Silver Falls? "Miss Hamilton, dear, that's a deadly serious—you can't possibly think—"

Grace let out a lilting laugh. "Oh, no, Mrs. Dinsby, not you! Never you! I was just asking a question, that's all." And then Grace did a strange thing. She looked right at Ben and held his gaze for several eternally long moments.

Ben felt all the air leave his body. She had noticed him at last. *This* was the sometime, *this* was the somewhere. Well, if she wanted to seek out and expose secret Communists, he could help her! They could be a team. And while they were keeping Silver Falls safe, she, of course, would fall in love with him. . . .

where panic, prejudice, suspicion, cowardice and demagogic

* * *

Before chorus practice with Mrs. Dinsby, he stood back and watched Grace with several of her best friends.

"Did you do the algebra?" Grace grabbed some papers from one of them. "I'll give it back in the morning, first thing. Don't tell my mother! She'll kill me!"

Then Grace caught sight of Ben again. He had to talk to her this time. But what would he say? *I don't care if you copy the algebra. I love you. I am tumble-toasted over you.*

She stared again, long and hard. Was she noticing (as he hoped she was) how his arms had gotten all big and solid? (Well, he had been doing extra push-ups every morning.) Or was she noticing (as he hoped she wasn't) the new rash of pimples on his chin? Did she like medium-height boys with dark blond hair, or did she prefer the tall, dark, handsome type?

She walked over to him, stood close as the air. He smelled perfume, very womanly. And she was taller than him, he suddenly realized, tall like her mother. He might have to adjust his fantasies. When he held her close, he was always the taller one.

"Um," he said.

"You have a secret, Benjamin Forster," she said, "and I know what it is!" Before Ben could say anything, Grace laughed, turned, and, ponytail bouncing, took her place with the sopranos.

They had to work on "The Star-Spangled Banner."

ambition constantly collided in a bedlam of recriminations.

Grace carried off the difficult high notes effortlessly. Ben was having trouble. *She knows! She knows how I feel. She thinks it's funny.*

"Mr. Forster!" Mrs. Dinsby glared at him.

He wanted to say, "My voice is changing." But what came out was, "My world is changing." It didn't matter, because he was mumbling and she didn't hear him, anyway.

"You're all over the place, Mr. Forster! Choose an octave and stay with it!"

Ben tried. *You have a secret. I know what it is.* Why would she say it like that?

"Mr. Forster." Mrs. Dinsby intensified her glare. "I want you to mouth the words. Do you understand? No sounds should come out of you."

He tried that, too. Just mouthing the words. But he couldn't do that, either. He wondered, vaguely, where those loud, screechy, unpleasant sounds were coming from.

"That's it!" Mrs. Dinsby said. "You're out!"

Outside in the too bright sunshine, Ben saw Mrs. Hamilton standing near her dark green convertible, the scarf around her neck fluttering like a flag. She was holding a batch of papers. As Ben passed her, he smelled perfume, the same as Grace's. He wanted to say, Why did your daughter say that to me? What did she mean? She's taller than you now, did you know that? She copies her algebra homework, did you know that, too?

The wealthiest, most secure nation in the world was sweat-

Instead, Mrs. Hamilton spoke to him. "Be sure to give this to your parents, young man." And she handed him a flyer. Another boy passed by, and she gave him one, too.

Ben couldn't read it in the glare. So he walked several blocks, past lovely homes with well-trimmed lawns and new cars in the garages, and stopped on a shady street.

DID YOU KNOW...?

appeared at the top of the page in big, dark letters.

1. That our very own town librarian, Mrs. Clara Forster, is a known Communist and must be removed from the Silver Falls Library so that another librarian, one with proven loyalties and no hidden agenda to influence young minds, may assume the position?

2. That removing her from her job will not violate her rights (either personal, legal, civil, or constitutional) in any way whatsoever?

Ben had to stop reading a moment. His hands were shaking.

Like hitchhikers who thumb rides only to rob and molest their benefactors, Communists have

drenched in fear. From New York to San Diego, from Seattle to been diabolically clever in appealing to our Christian-like qualities, to our softheartedness, our kindness. Thus, anyone who tries to remove security risks from sensitive positions is blasted as un-Christian.

Mrs. Forster is by no means the only security risk working or living in this immediate neighborhood. You can discourage subversives from settling here by signing the letter below. You have nothing to fear if you sign, but will probably have many heartaches later on if you don't. Please, also, send us the names and addresses of your friends who have not yet signed. Let's keep our community free of subversives! Cut off and sign the letter below the dotted line, NOW. Mail it to me, TODAY.

From the ALERTED AMERICANS GROUP, Mrs. Eleanor Hamilton, Silver Falls, Pa.

This was the letter below the dotted line:

To restore peace and harmony to the Silver Falls area, won't the trustees of the Silver Falls Library please replace the present librarian, Mrs. Clara Forster, with someone of unquestioned loyalty? Thank you.

Miami, federal, state and municipal employees worried about

To restore peace and harmony? But that was why Ben and his mother had moved here in the first place!

According to the piece of paper Ben held in his hands, his mother was...the enemy. And the person fighting for freedom was...Grace's mother.

He looked through the leafy trees up at the cloudless sky. Please, he prayed, let a bomb fall on me right now.

When he got home, he didn't use the front door. Instead, he went in through the back porch.

"Benny, is that you?" His mother, home early. "We've got to talk about something."

They sat at the kitchen table. Before she could say anything, Ben handed her the flyer.

"What is that?" she said.

"I was going to ask you."

His mother read it quietly, calmly. All she did was slowly shake her head.

Ben looked at her straight dark hair, pulled back, her long face, sharp blue eyes, simple blue dress. *This is my mother*, he told himself. *Western Pennsylvania Librarian of the Year, three years in a row.*

When she finished, she put it facedown on the table. "I wanted to talk to you first, but I suppose Eleanor Hamilton has been a busy little bee, reading the morning paper, writing this up, and copying it, all in one day. I know her, Benny. She comes to the library sometimes, complains about books, tries to get them banned. She won beauty pageants as a teenager. Then she became a big-deal golf player."

"National champion," Ben said. He knew, because of Grace.

"So now she's not a beauty queen or a golf champion anymore. So now she has nothing else to do, except try to destroy books—and people, too, I suppose."

"Why does she want to destroy you?"

Now it was his mother's turn to give him something to read. Page eleven of the *Pittsburgh Post-Gazette*.

What caught his eye was an advertisement. *It's here from Philco . . . a refrigerator so completely automatic, IT THINKS FOR ITSELF!* "You want a new refrigerator? One that can think?"

"Look." She pointed to a one-sentence paragraph near the end of an article. "Mr. Henry Allbright, of Boston, Massachusetts, cited Professor Barney Steig, of Riverton College, in Illinois, and Mrs. Clara Forster, now a librarian in Silver Falls, Pennsylvania, as having been members of Communist Party 'cells' in 1947."

Ben had to read this single sentence many times before the words straightened themselves out and he could understand them. 1947. He was—what, five, six, seven years old? He couldn't even do the math. *Think*, he told himself. Even refrigerators can think.

"Henry Allbright," he said. "I know that name."

"He worked undercover for the FBI. There's a TV show based on the people he turned in. *I Wore Three Hats for the FBI*."

ssociations, and hoped that the letter from the loyalty

"I love that show!" Ben said, though it seemed wildly off the point. "You knew him?"

"Back in Riverton. He's not a good person, Benny. He was saying things about me then, too. It's part of why we moved."

"It's why we moved? Why didn't you tell me?"

"You were so young. It didn't seem important, to burden you with that."

Not important, to move from one part of the country to another? "What *else* didn't you tell me?"

She started to say something, stopped, and started again. "Benny, there's a difference—how do I explain it? Sometimes I've kept things to myself. Things that were part of my life, things that didn't need to be part of yours."

He nodded, understood. He didn't spill everything to her, either. The way he felt about Grace, for instance. Still, even now. "So, okay, who's this professor guy?"

"Never heard of him."

This is my mother. Ben breathed in deeply. *She makes tuna casseroles with onion rings. There's one in the oven right now; I can smell it already.*

"I heard it on the radio last night—that Henry Allbright testified yesterday, or maybe the day before. I figured it would make the papers—maybe today, maybe tomorrow." She took a deep breath, too. "I got a subpoena at work, Benny. Next week, I have to go to Washington, D.C., to testify. They'll put me under oath, ask me questions. Questions about whether or not I was ever a Communist."

board would never come." —David Caute, *The Great Fear: The*

Washington, D.C. *From one total-destruction circle to another.* "What will you tell them?"

"I'll tell them, in so many words, that it's none of their business."

"You can't say that! You have to say that you weren't!"

"Benny—"

"You could lose your job!" He had heard stories, what happened to people who wouldn't answer questions. "You could go to jail!"

"*Benny.* They have no right to ask me, just because somebody accuses me. Somebody like Henry Allbright, who loves attention and eats it up with a spoon."

"Mom, listen." He had to make her understand. "Just mouth the words. I do it all the time in chorus." He said it for her silently: "*I am not a Communist. I never was.*"

"No, Benny."

"Just mouth the words, but put some sound in, enough so they can hear you."

She shook her head.

He hated it, that he started to cry. She might lose her job. She might go to jail. It was too terrible! And what would happen to him? How could he think this was a war without casualties or victims, without real bombs bursting, *snap, crackle, pop*? Should he duck under the kitchen table, cover his head? "Mom. Tell me. I'm not the government. I won't tell a soul. Are you a Communist?" Even as he said it, he knew it sounded crazy. Why would his mother want to take over Silver Falls, only to drop a bomb on it?

Anti-Communist Purge Under Truman and Eisenhower (6)

"I'm not a Communist, Benny. I love this country. I'm a loyal, patriotic American."

Ben blinked at her. "So what's the problem?"

"The problem is, they're going to ask me about the past, before we came here. I won't answer about that."

He tried to remember, back in Riverton. After his father died, his mother was . . . well, busy. She'd gone back to school and become a librarian. Was there other stuff going on, too? He had no idea. "Well," he said, "*were* you?"

"I'm not going to answer you, either."

"Oh, thanks a heap!"

"It's better this way. This way, what's important is that your mother has a right to privacy, and she's fighting for that right, even if it takes months, or years."

Ben felt the room tilt, almost as if he were becoming aware, for the first time, that the earth spun on its axis. It had always been true, that the earth did this. The difference was, now he felt it. He held on to the table, to steady himself.

"So, okay, while all this is happening, what do I do? Wait, to see if you lose your job? Wait, to see if you go to jail? Hold my breath—for months, or years?"

Yes, that was exactly what he had to do.

Things Happen

Lisa Rowe Fraustino

The first thing that happened in 1968 was Sunshine Shaffmaster drowned.

From the time we learned to toddle, Sunshine and I were inseparable friends. Her real name was Lois Ann. Sunshine came from her personality, unlike my nickname, Jacket, which had blurred from Jacqueline Kathleen. I was the only child in a big house that stood in the middle of our family business, a junkyard that ran for acres. Sunshine lived in a little house full of teenage brothers. Her favorite was Francis, the eldest, the only one who never played practical jokes on her. My favorite was Edward, the middlest, a tall, hairy version of Sunshine, complete with long red ponytail, green eyes as bright as the ocean on a sunny day, and a face more freckled than not. He had a sticky-outy singing voice that always made me laugh. He was also an artist, the kind whose paintings always made you think, then smile when you figured them out.

Sunshine and I did everything together. Our favorite activity used to be playing imagination games with storybook characters, but now that we were twelve going on thirteen, we spent more time imagining what it would be like to french a boy.

Everyone said that the accident wasn't my fault, that things just happen. But it was my idea to play Whip. We were all out on the lake on New Year's Day, Sunshine's family and mine, skating, sledding, cooking over a bonfire, living life to the fullest, for the moment, trying not to think about the fact that Francis had completed basic training and would be flying off to Vietnam the next day. The ice wasn't safe near the docks, so we started our game way out in the middle, where the ice was a foot thick. Nobody realized how close to the edge we'd spun. Someone let go of me. Sunshine's mitten came off in my hand as I tumbled to my seat. She stayed on her feet and sailed on, squealing with glee until the ice started to crack and her glee turned to terror.

The second thing that happened that year was I lost my voice. I couldn't even yell for help when I saw Sunshine go through the ice. I was frozen in place, hanging on to her warm mitten while the other kids were all whipping the other way obliviously. Francis was roasting a hot dog on the shore and saw everything. He threw down his stick and charged across the ice, stripping off his snowsuit as he ran, and dove in after her like a true hero.

To witness your best friend die at the age of twelve is not pleasant. I've had my voice back for a long time but still can't talk about the rest.

The third thing that happened that year was that Francis came home from Vietnam in March. Soldiers sent off to war don't usually come right back. If they do, the lucky ones come back in bandages. The unlucky ones come back in coffins. It wasn't a lucky year.

Actually, I shouldn't call it a war, since the United States never officially declared war against Vietnam. Officially, it was a conflict. U.S. politicians had this idea that it would be a disaster to allow Communism to spread, so we took sides to stop it in the civil war between North and South Vietnam. It wasn't like our own Civil War, where everyone had to take sides because it was our own country we were fighting for, and in. It was confusing.

Those spring days after Francis died passed like rain on a window, the drops distinct at the moment they hit the pane, then blurring together in streaks and finally rushing into one mad torrent down the gutter. When I wasn't in school or in a doctor's office playing games that were supposed to bring my voice back, I stayed in my room having tea parties for storybook characters who filled my head with chatter that nobody else could hear. I wanted to talk with real people. I just couldn't. I kept a notebook and pencil in my pocket to communicate if pointing and mouthing words didn't work.

Summer came, and each raindrop day brought a new storm of words and pictures into the house through the black-and-white television in our living room. Martin Luther King Jr. assassinated, and then Bobby Kennedy, too . . . race riots sweeping the nation . . . students taking over the universities . . . presidential campaigns full of chaos . . . hippies and yippies protesting the draft that forced young

It is estimated that seven hundred thousand men were drafted

men to go fight in the war, and Dr. Spock indicted for help-
ing them...and every day that terrible body count of soldiers killed in Vietnam.

Every day, when I heard the body count through the
heating vent to my room, I thought of Francis and time
moved backward until he was diving into the icy water and I
was sitting at the sharp-toothed edge of ice, frozen in place,
staring at Sunshine's mitten with a shadowy sense of someone
hovering over me, until I realized it was just my mother
bringing me my dessert. She and my father always had theirs
on TV trays in front of the news.

Once school let out and the weather warmed, I spent
more and more time in the junkyard instead of my room.
The doctors had told my parents that nothing was wrong
with my voice box, that I'd talk when I was ready, so they
didn't worry at me about my silence. They did worry about
my safety, alone in the junkyard with dangerous broken glass
and rust and strangers wandering about looking for gas caps
and carburetors. I had to follow three rules. One: Wear a
whistle around my neck to blow loudly in case of trouble.
Two: Never go past the rope they put up to mark the
Forbidden Zone, where the sound of the whistle wouldn't
reach the house. Three: Always be home in time for dinner.

I had no desire to wander far from the watchful eyes of
the gabled house anyhow, and I liked the whistle around my
neck like a portable scream, but the dinner deadline gave me
some trouble. My imaginary friends had no sense of time. Not
that time mattered anyway. Even my thirteenth birthday

blurred into the other summer days just like another raindrop in a puddle. I spent it in a Jeep with the only gift that meant anything to me, a box of Sunshine's books from the Shaffmasters.

Edward, who delivered the books, had sung in his sticky-outy voice a silly invitation to go for banana splits, an old ritual he had with Sunshine. My taste buds would have liked to go, but my head shook itself no. It was too difficult looking at him, with his long, straight red hair, green eyes as bright as the ocean on a sunny day, and a face more freckled than not. I still adored Edward. I just couldn't stop thinking that he wasn't Sunshine.

September came flowing along, and with it the bus to school. I was very good at school but disliked it because it required me to sit among real kids who taunted me when the teacher's back was turned. They'd always called me Junkyard Jackie; now it gave them pleasure to rhyme it with wacky.

When I got home that first day of school, I flung my book bag on the porch and ran straight to the little purple Volkswagen with rust polka dots Sunshine had dubbed Beetle Bug, our favorite place to play Cram-the-Characters-In. The point of the game was to imagine how many protagonists could fit inside. Today I saved Stuart Little and Thumbelina for last. They sat in Babar's nostrils and got sneezed onto the roof of a tractor-trailer zooming along the new interstate highway that ran alongside the junkyard.

While they were hitchhiking home, I realized it was two minutes before dinner.

Sprinting houseward like Peter Pan from the crocodile, I smacked into a man. My hand went to the whistle I always wore around my neck.

"Oh!" he said, and I thought the same thing, and then he said the next thing I was thinking, "I'm sorry, I didn't see you—" and then we both realized we recognized each other. "Jacket, what are you doing here!" he said while I thought, *Edward, what are you doing here!* The surprise of seeing that unexpected freckle face in the junkyard, at that very moment when I was late for dinner, knocked the breath out of me as much as the collision.

He yanked my braid. I punched his shoulder.

"Dinner?" I mouthed, pointing to the house.

He shook his head wildly. "No, no, really, I can't. I'm really just, uh..." He sounded so incredibly nervous that I wondered if something was wrong. "I'm hiding out here for a while—hanging out, I mean—to, ah...paint. Paint the junkyard. Pictures of it. Paintings. Tragic irony."

Luckily my parents were discussing politics and didn't notice I was late. My father was a Republican and in favor of stopping this fiddling around in Vietnam. He thought we should give our boys permission to pull out all the stops and win the war so all those American lives wouldn't be lost in vain. My mother was a Democrat and also in favor of stopping all the fiddling around in Vietnam. She thought we should pull out all of our troops immediately and stop sacrificing teenage boys for a cause that wasn't any of our business.

My father said, "I suppose World War II wasn't our

or evading induction was a fine of ten thousand dollars and five business, either? I suppose you'd just as soon have Nazis as Communists take over the world with Russia in charge?"

My mother said, "It's USSR, not Russia. World War II wasn't a civil war, we gladly fought it to save our allies, and the average age of soldiers was twenty-six, not nineteen, like now," and he said, and she said, and so on and on, until it was time for the news. I was heading upstairs to get Mary Poppins to help me with my homework when a local reporter said, "Vietnam draft protesters campaign for peace at the statehouse. . . ." Background voices were singing "All You Need Is Love," one male voice sticking out like the cherry on a banana split.

I'd have recognized that sticky-outy voice anywhere. It was my favorite Shaffmaster brother, whom I just so happened to have bumped into less than an hour earlier. Edward was on TV! How groovy! I stopped on the stairs and snapped around to look, just in time to see a young man with a long ponytail push aside an anti-antiwar protester's sign that said COWARDS. Then Edward lifted a piece of paper to the camera and ripped it into shreds.

"Shave and a haircut, two bits," my father sang. He did that whenever he saw a hippie, even ones like Edward who were well groomed and wore Clean for Gene buttons because Eugene McCarthy wanted to end the armed conflict and they wanted him to be president.

"That boy looks familiar," said my mother. "Why, it's—"

"For Pete's sake, you're right, it is," my father said in amazement.

"Uncle Sam!" Edward shouted to the camera. "Thanks for the invitation to your war party, but I'm going to have to RSVP my regrets!" You could tell his face was angry red, even though the TV was black-and-white.

"Oh no!" my mother exclaimed. "He's ripped up his draft papers! He'll go to jail!"

My parents were still sitting behind their TV trays, their mouths hanging open with no dessert or coffee going in and no more words coming out. My bones melted out from under me, and I flopped on the stairs. My mother came and put her arm around me, swaying like in a rocking chair. We sat like that until a soap commercial came on and my bones hardened.

I didn't sleep much that night, worrying about Edward. I couldn't bear the thought of his going to jail, or going to Vietnam and maybe coming back right away, either in bandages or in a box. I wasn't going to let anything happen to another one of Sunshine's brothers. I wasn't!

The next morning I gobbled breakfast and ran out to see if Edward was still around where I'd bumped into him. Sure enough, I found him curled up in the back of a Chevy van, sound asleep, looking too young and sweet to be a fugitive. He had nothing with him except his usual knapsack with art supplies poking out of the crannies. Silently I propped my lunch bag at his waist, wished him happy dreams, and turned to leave, but something pulled on my elbow sleeve.

"Wait. I need to tell you why I'm here," Edward said hoarsely, his eyes still shut. "I'm—"

I pulled on his beard so he'd open his eyes, and I mouthed, "I know."

"You know?"

I got out my notebook. *It was on the news.*

"The news!" He sat up, his face crunched like a totaled car. "Oh, why did I have to be so dumb? The draft notice came right before the rally, and I was so angry that when I saw the camera, something wild came over me. I ripped up the notice, hopped on Harley Baby, and rode." He nodded toward a big pine where I saw his Harley-Davidson motorcycle hiding under the branches. "I thought I'd split for Canada, but then I thought how sad the family would be after—"

He gulped, looking sidelong at me. I nodded understandingly.

"Make love, not war, man. So I came here to hang until I could figure out what to do next. And now that I've been on the news, I can't even go to town for a tube of toothpaste without being hauled away."

I wrote, *I'm gonna hold your hand,* like the Beatles song, only without the *wanna.*

Edward shook his head like a dog out of water. "Uh-unh. You're not getting involved, except to look the other way for a few days while I decide what next. Do your own thing."

I already am. Toothpaste. What else?

Very stubbornly, I stared him down. With a defeated sort of smile, he took my pencil. He chewed the end a moment and looked up as if to find his list written in the limbs of the spindly trees that had grown up between the junk heaps.

Soap, Water, Towel, Food, Candles, Matches. Then he chewed the end of the pencil some more and added *Newspaper*.

With a grimace he handed me the list. "I feel terrible letting you do this."

You're welcome.

As I gathered the rations that day after school, my heart beat double time, but my nervousness was for nothing. My mother didn't take a second look at my lumpy book bag when I left the house, merely reminded me to whistle if I got into any trouble.

The moment I dumped the bag into what Edward was now calling his Van Sweet Van, he scrambled for yesterday's newspaper and read it hungrily. Then he got out his art knife and started cutting the news apart, pasting words onto a piece of paper. When he finished, he handed me a note: *Do not worry about the guy with red hair. He is safe and dry and full of food.*

"Can you get this to Lester at school tomorrow?" he asked. Lester was the youngest of the Shaffmaster brothers.

So the next morning before class, I went to the eighth-grade wing to spy out Lester's locker, then later got a bathroom pass and sneaked over to slip the secret message through a slot in his locker when nobody was looking. My heart beat quadruple time. I think all those heartbeats must have used up an extra day of my life, but it was worth it to feel alive.

No longer did time flow like rain. It had crystallized into unique memories about taking care of Edward. In the crisp, getting-shorter autumn days that followed, I spent all of my precious time after school with him and neglected my imaginary friends. I always took him a snack—fruit, cookies, peanut butter sandwiches. One afternoon while my mother was combing through the kitchen to make her weekly grocery-shopping list, she held up the last carrot and said, "Skinny Minnie must have a tapeworm. I can't keep the larder full anymore!" She seemed pleased, actually, since I'd lost my appetite along with my voice. I smiled with embarrassment, snatched the carrot, and bit off the tip. The rest went in my pocket for Edward.

She was also pleased that I volunteered to clean up after dinner each night. I did it so I could sneak all the leftovers out to Edward along with the newspaper, which I stole out of the garbage, even the pages my mother had used to wrap up the vegetable peels. He didn't want to miss a word.

Our biggest problem was water. I wasn't strong enough to carry jugs with enough for Edward to drink, cook, and bathe. One evening when my father was hosing the daily dust off his car, I realized that Edward could come hose for himself while everyone slept. He did that, and I continued to sneak occasional messages to Lester, and all was well, until one night a few weeks after Edward starred in the evening news, when my mother pushed away her emptied dinner plate and said, "I'm in the mood for a sundae. Let's go to the ice cream parlor."

"But we'll miss Walter Cronkite." Walter Cronkite was my father's favorite newscaster. "And the raisin pie." Pie was

U.S. Attorneys for prosecution on draft law violations. Of these, not his favorite dessert, but when his routine was upset, so was he.

"Raisin pie is always better the second day," my mother replied, "and the news is never much good. We're in a rut behind our TV trays. Let's be spontaneous for a change."

Father grumbled the whole way there about getting spontaneous dust on his car after he'd already hosed it down for the night, but once the sundaes came, glopped with chocolate and heaped with whipped cream, he pronounced Monday Sundae Day.

"Doesn't that defeat the point of being spontaneous?" my mother said.

I finished my last drip of chocolate sauce and gazed out the window, wondering which of the cars in the parking lot would wind up at the junkyard someday and feeling sorry for Edward, alone back there in the dark. As if my thoughts had conjured him up, a big Harley-Davidson motorcycle covered with stickers of flowers and peace signs came roaring into the parking lot. The driver had on a frayed jean jacket with white bleach splotches just like Edward's, too, and a Clean for Gene political button. The girl climbing off the back and shaking her hair free of her fluorescent swirly-colored bandanna looked just like Edward's high school sweetheart, Debbie Somethingorother. I had fond memories of his brothers teasing them unmercifully whenever they tried to make out in the darkened TV room at the Shaffmasters'.

Their faces tipped together. I'd recognize that outline anywhere. It was them! Edward and Debbie Somethingorother!

twenty-five thousand were indicted, and about nine thousand men

Really! I pulled back from the window in alarm, as if by some chance watching Edward would cause others to watch him, too, and recognize him, and call the police, and haul him off to jail, or to the armed conflict. How could he leave the junkyard and risk his safety? Oh, Edward, I thought. You are no coward. You are too brave for your own good.

Or stupid, my mother seemed to say.

Yes. Stupid, and selfish, and—what? How could my mother jump in on my thoughts? I must have heard wrong. I gave her a puzzled look.

"I said it's too bad," my mother explained, "about Bobby Kennedy being assassinated, like his brother. He would have won the presidency and ended the war, too."

"Ended the war without winning, you mean?" said my father. "What's the use of that?"

"Their poor mother," said mine, avoiding a fight. "Well, we'd best be getting home."

That night I lay awake, worrying my anger away, watching the shadows shift on the wall, listening to night sounds—the scratch of limbs against the house, an occasional hoot of an owl, trucks rumbling on the interstate. Finally, faintly, I heard the distant *putter-putter* of Harley Baby moving through the junkyard. It blinked out like a light and finally, faintly, I slept.

All the next day I carried a pit of worry in my stomach. What a relief it was when after school I found Edward sitting behind an easel not far from an ambulance that had been in an accident on the way to an accident. Next to him on the ground lay the finished ambulance picture, painted in splotches of color a shade or two away from real. Now he was drawing an empty mayonnaise jar next to a pail on a stump. None of the lines met, so the drawing had an empty, cutoff feeling to it. The way an empty jar, an empty pail, and a stump ought to feel! I liked the drawing so much that I spontaneously patted Edward's shoulder.

He shrieked with surprise and jolted. His pencil went flying.

"Jacket, don't sneak up on me like that. Man, you scared the shinola out of me."

"Sorry," I mouthed.

Now he smiled. "Glad you like it."

On my notebook, I wrote quickly, *Last night I saw something I didn't like.*

He looked at me warily. "What do you mean?"

Banana split?

He crammed his eyes shut and turned in a circle. When he faced me, he looked at my ear instead of into my eyes. "Whoops. I'm not a very cooperative fugitive, am I? It's just that I miss everyone, and Debbie keeps after me to—"

No! I tried to say. How can you stand here making excuses when Sunshine drowned and I lost my voice and Francis came home in a coffin already this year? Don't enough bad things just happen without you inviting more? Instead of all that, though, a little burpy noise came out of my throat. It was the closest thing to a word that I'd spoken since "Let's play Whip."

Edward looked shocked at me, looked ashamed at his feet,

then looked sweetly into my eyes. "You're right. It was dumb. I'm really sorry. I promise I won't sneak out to see Deb anymore. Are we cool?" He looked so much like Sunshine at that moment, I wished we hadn't gone for the spontaneous sundae so I wouldn't have found out that he'd been sneaking around and I wouldn't know to be mad at him. I forgave him. But the pit of worry stayed put, and I carried it in my stomach until a few days later when I got to Van Sweet Van to find Harley Baby loaded down like a pack mule and Edward holding up his hands in self-defense.

"Before you get all helter-skelter," he said, "everything's hip. You don't have to be responsible for me anymore. Just this once, I went to sell enough artwork to stock up on food, clothes, blankets, a gas heater for the cold weather, and a new toothbrush to go with my toothpaste. Everything I need to take care of myself! And I'm moving to a better place to do it. It's really *cool*. Come on, you'll see." He gestured for me to climb on his lap, which was the only spot left to sit. I did, and we puttered up the hill through decades of junk, straight to the Forbidden Zone.

"Can you climb down and hold that rope up high while I scoot under?" he asked.

I grasped the whistle that dangled from a piece of yarn around my neck beneath my windbreaker and turned to look back at the house, which had sunk behind a ridge of junk until all that showed was the dark slate roof, glowering at me like a knit brow. As I slipped off Edward's lap, I remembered the day my father had strung the mile of clothesline around

and prosecuted for desertion. By 1970, ten percent of cases

junk and trees, how I'd gone with him blowing my whistle toward the house, how my mother had stood on the porch blowing her whistle back at me.

"Nobody will ever find me!" Edward was saying. He looked so happy. Being with him made me happy. How could I tell him I couldn't go with him past the rope? I pulled my windbreaker strings snug around my chin, as if tightening my determination, and lifted the rope, then dropped it like hot electric wire the moment Harley Baby's taillight blinked past.

"Ashes to ashes, iron to rust," Edward said. This was the overgrown part of the junkyard my great-grandfather had started decades earlier, and it was slow going. At last Edward cut the engine and gestured toward a mound of mountain laurels surrounding what looked like a big white box. "Welcome to my new Home Sweet Ice Truck Away from Van."

Cool it was! Once when I asked my father why he called the refrigerator an icebox, he'd explained how huge chunks of ice used to be cut from the lake in winter, then stored deep in the sawdust of barns to be delivered in the summer to houses that had insulated chests to chill food.

Edward's new hideout was secluded, well camouflaged, comfortable. Clearly he was well out of harm's way, and taking care of him was no longer my concern. So why wouldn't the fear leave my stomach even for a moment, or the guilt leave my heart when I crossed into the Forbidden Zone to take Edward his daily newspaper?

I'd learned that things happen. That was why.

The first Tuesday in November, the teacher handed out mock election ballots for president, saying, "Children tend to vote like their families, so today the school will probably predict the real outcome at the polls." My parents were canceling each other out, my father voting for Richard Nixon and my mother for Hubert Humphrey. I didn't know whose side to take, so I wrote in Eugene McCarthy for Edward. Richard Nixon won by a landslide.

When I got home that day, a police car was parked in the driveway, and the policemen themselves, two of them, were on the front porch with my mother. My father always stayed in the office until precisely five o'clock. "Jacket, come sit down, honey," she said. "These nice policemen want to ask you about Sunshine's brother."

I couldn't sit. The pit in my stomach felt like it was spinning up through my guilty heart into my head. What I had dreaded all these weeks was coming true.

The first officer began in a kindly voice, "I believe you know an Edward Shaffmaster? Sorry to say, he's a fugitive from the law. He was sighted protesting the draft at the election polls today, and we tracked him to the interstate exit near here before we lost him. Now we suspect that he's hiding out in this junkyard. Have you seen him at all in the past few weeks?"

What a relief! They hadn't found him yet. There was still time to warn him. I should shake my head. I had to shake my head. The only safe answer was a quick and unmistakable *no*.

But my head wouldn't shake. *Sneaking* I could do for a cause. I wasn't accustomed to *lying to the police*.

"I take it you have? Seen him?" the second officer said.

I nodded instinctively. So dizzy, so confused. How could Edward go to another protest?

The policemen exchanged smiles. The first one pulled a pencil and pad out of his pocket. "Where, exactly, did you see him? And when?"

I gulped and looked at my mother. She ran her hand gently through my hair and smiled a sad smile with shaky lips. Our eyes connected and held, speaking volumes. In that moment, I realized that my mother knew that Edward was in the junkyard. Her glistening eyes seemed to say, So that's where the carrots went. You don't have to tell them. I'm behind you.

The dizziness whipped out of my head, and with it spun away the fear and the guilt. I took the officer's pencil and wrote slowly, calmly, *Parking lot, Sweetie's Ice Cream Shoppe, one Monday night.*

The second officer suddenly seemed shorter. "Not here? Not in the junkyard?"

My mother cleared her throat, nodded. "That makes sense. I didn't see Edward there that night, but I saw his girlfriend, alone, ordering two banana splits to go."

The officers looked confused at each other. The second officer said, "Shaffmaster's got a chick?" Then he looked excited. "What's her name?"

My mother smiled. "We always called her Debbie

Somethingorother. Edward's parents would know."

The officers snorted wryly at each other. The first one said, "Those Shaffmasters all have amnesia about Edward. They can't even remember what bed he slept in."

While I was trying not to smile at that, my mother put on a stern face. "Now that you've asked your questions," she said, crossing her arms, "I'm going to have to ask you gentlemen to leave."

"I'm sorry, ma'am, but we can't do that until we've finished searching the premises," the first officer said in a high voice, like he was talking to a little kid.

"I didn't think you could do that without a search warrant, sir. Not if you aren't sure that he's here. Nobody saw him enter this property, correct?"

The second officer sighed himself even shorter. "If we lose the element of surprise, he'll get away. Do you really want to let these subversive draft dodgers shirk their duty and tear this country apart? Do you really wish to obstruct justice?"

"Life goes on, gentlemen," said my mother, "and there are lots more important things in it than politics. They're called people."

The officers looked angry enough to pop. "All right, Mrs. Alexander, have it your way," the first one said. "We'll be back with the search warrant. But if Shaffmaster escapes while we're gone, you'll have that weight on your conscience."

"It'll weigh a lot more if he doesn't," she whispered as their car wheels crunched away.

men and women moved to Canada to protest the war and escape

A few minutes later, I was going under the rope again, only this time my mother was with me, looking determined. We were breathless by the time we reached the little copse of mountain laurels. The ice-truck door was open, and Edward's things were strewn about, making the place look very lived-in, but he wasn't around. I sat on his cot to catch my breath, each heartbeat a stab of panic through my heart. Where was he? His knapsack full of art supplies was gone. Was he out working? Except where was his sleeping bag? And the winter parka that should be hanging on the hook next to the door? And no toothbrush, either. I knew what that meant. He'd gone away.

My mother picked up a tube of toothpaste. "Same kind we use!" She winked, teasing, as she reached for the single piece of art Edward had left facedown on his makeshift plywood drawing table. She turned it over and sighed. "He really is gifted," she said. "It would be a shame for that talent to go to waste. Have you seen this?" She held the painting out to me.

"Oh!" I gasped in surprise at the picture, which I had not seen, and then I said, "Oh!" again from surprise at the first "oh" coming out through my voice box. He'd left me a gift.

The painting showed a big, bright world of grass and flowers and trees with me in the middle, big face smiling and big hand waving up out of the page with a little body barely showing underneath, standing inside the shadow of a cloud. Overhead, a girl-shaped cloud with Sunshine's face was flying off the page, the sun beaming all around her. The picture filled me with warmth, as if Sunshine was alive inside me. And, of course, she was. I'd just never realized it before.

One last thing happened in 1968. The mailman brought me a letter on December 31, postmarked from Canada. It said, in cut-and-pasted newspaper letters, *Peace*.

Faizabad Harvest, 1980

Suzanne Fisher Staples

When our father and the other men of Faizabad joined the *mujahideen* at the start of the war, it fell to my twelve-year-old brother, Hassan, to look after our family of six. Sometimes he tested his authority by ordering our older sister, Amina, around until she grew angry.

"Bring me water," Hassan said to Amina one afternoon when he came in from watering the squash vines in the field. It was autumn, nearly harvest time.

"Get it yourself," said Amina, who was busy making bread. "I'm preparing your dinner, and I don't have time to bring water." She slapped the brown dough from one hand to the other emphatically, turning it until it made a round, flat disk. Raising one eyebrow and eyeing Hassan sharply, she threaded the bread onto a long metal hook and lowered it into the mud oven. She looked downward only to adjust the stone in front of the damper so the fire burned hotter. Then she reached out and tore off another handful of dough, dismissing Hassan the way our mother dismissed the younger children.

Amina was fifteen, and it was hard for her to obey the boy whose bottom she'd wiped when she was only four

More than one and a half million people died during the fighting years old. She had helped our mother look after us younger children—Hassan, me, Farida, and Ahmed—for years before the Soviet infidels invaded Afghanistan and turned our lives upside down.

I went on stirring potatoes and onions over the fire. I watched from behind the curls of spicy smoke that drifted upward from the pan to see what Hassan would do. He stood behind Amina for a moment, studying her back. He reached out carefully and yanked a strand of her hair so that the knot she tied it in to keep it from her face unraveled into a silky stream that spilled darkly over her shoulders. Hassan ducked out of the dimly lit kitchen through the curtained doorway to get his own drink of water from the well.

"That troublemaker Hedayat is a bad influence on him," Amina said under her breath, rewinding her hair. Hedayat was our cousin. He also was fifteen, and he was impatient to join the *mujahideen*, the Afghan freedom fighters. He bossed everyone, including Hassan, and generally made a nuisance of himself because he wanted to fight the Soviets and his father would not allow it.

"Allah does not want such young martyrs," our father had said when Hassan—who was just two years older than I— asked if he could join the *mujahideen*. And everyone knew there weren't enough guns. The eldest sons of the village stayed behind to mind the farms and look after their families while the men fought.

Our mother came in then and stacked her baskets against the wall. She sighed and took a red clay jar of water back out through the doorway to wash her hands in the courtyard.

"Go with Ahdi and take her a towel," said Amina, tilting her head at me. I lifted the pan from the fire and propped the wooden spoon against the edge. Then I put the kettle on for tea and followed my mother outside.

I took the clay jar from her and poured water over her hands as she washed away the dust and sticky juice from the grapes she'd sold in the market. She splashed a handful of the water onto her face. I handed her the towel, and when she took it away from drying her face, she was smiling.

My mother was beautiful when she smiled. Her eyes were dark, and they crinkled up at the edges. Her full brown lips showed every one of her perfect, square white teeth.

"That's better," she said, leaning forward to take my face between her hands and cover it with kisses. Our mother loved to gather her children around her to talk at the end of the day, to hug us and kiss us repeatedly. She did it even more after our father went to war. She tightened the strings of love around us to keep us safe, as if it would save him, too. "Where are Farida and Ahmed?"

"They're bringing firewood," I answered, handing her a chipped glass filled with cool water. "Tea will be ready soon."

After dinner, when the sun fell below the horizon and the dry air cooled, Amina and I went with Farida, who was seven, to pick more grapes for our mother to take to market in the city of Kandahar the next morning. The dust was chalky between our toes, still warm from the afternoon sun. The sky was a brilliant blue overhead, like lapis lazuli, with a few stars sparkling bravely, more stars each time we looked up. The horizon was the color of pale apricots near the place where the sun had set.

We laughed and teased Farida, who had been stung by a bee that afternoon. She had shrieked and shrieked until Amina came running with a cup of cool water, which she poured over the sting. Amina had plucked the barb out with her fingernails. She spat in the powdery dirt to make a poultice that she packed on Farida's ankle, which swelled to nearly twice its normal size. Farida sniffled, and Amina sang softly to calm her. By dinnertime Farida had forgotten the sting, and she ate as if nothing at all had happened to her.

"I thought it was at least a cobra, perhaps even a leopard," said Amina, who had difficulty keeping her face serious while her eyes twinkled like the early stars. Farida smiled shyly and hid her eyes behind her arm.

Our bellies were full and we were happy as we snipped heavy bunches of the small purple grapes that were our livelihood. We laid them carefully in wide, flat baskets that our mother would carry stacked on her head the five miles to Kandahar just after dawn the next day.

I looked up at Amina just as her eyes narrowed and her lips parted in the glimmering afterglow of day, and just before I heard—or felt in my chest, rather—the rhythmic thumping of the blades of the helicopter gunship before it slipped over the top of the hill. Without speaking, Amina dropped her scissors and grapes and grabbed Farida and me, each by a wrist, and the three of us ran down the path and into the courtyard of our house.

Ahdi sat on a wood cot in the courtyard bathing our little brother, Ahmed. His delicate shoulder blades stuck out like the wings of a baby chick as she rubbed a wet cloth over them. I wondered whether there was time to gather the laundry drying on sticks beside the wall and take it inside so the dust wouldn't spoil it. At the time those few frantic seconds felt like lazy hours, before I grabbed up Ahmed, who squealed, thinking I was playing a game.

Ahdi went back to pick up a shawl to wrap Ahmed against the night chill. Amina screamed at her to come now. At the same moment she shoved me roughly in the middle of my back so that I nearly fell, and that was when our house exploded.

Time unfolded in tiny, ragged segments that seemed to last small eternities. I felt myself being lifted into the air with Ahmed in my arms. At the same time I felt a tremendous pressure inside my ears, but heard nothing, and it seemed the whole world had erupted silently into flames of orange-and-black smoke.

The next thing I remembered was crumpling to the ground, still holding Ahmed, and turning to where Ahdi stood, her face frozen, mouth open, as if she wanted to speak. Instead of words, a thick stream of black blood gushed from her lips. The long metal hook Amina had hung the bread on in the oven protruded from Ahdi's chest.

Hassan grabbed Ahmed from me, and screamed at us to

run for the underground irrigation tunnels. I thought I'd mis-
heard him and turned back to help Ahdi. But Hassan pushed
me as Amina had done, and I wondered if Amina was dead,
too, as I ran for the irrigation tunnels.

When we were safe underground, I looked desperately for
Amina in the dim lantern light that flickered on the walls. I
climbed over people huddled beside the trickle of water at
the bottom of the tunnel. Many were spattered with blood.
They sat, not speaking, some of them coughing or moaning.
I stepped on the hand of an elder, who cursed, but I kept
searching for Amina.

I found her washing blood from Farida's face with the
hem of her tunic. Blood also oozed from Amina's nose, and
she wiped at it absently with the back of her hand. I realized
that I still held the washcloth Ahdi had used to bathe
Ahmed just moments before. I handed it to Amina.

Amina's eyes filled with tears when she looked up at me.
I sat beside her and put my arms around her shoulders and laid
my head against her neck. Amina stroked my hair as grief
convulsed my body. Over the next hour the ground jumped
beneath us and dirt trickled down from the roof of the ancient
irrigation tunnels that had been built by our grandfathers'
grandfathers to keep the water from being sucked up by the
mountain desert air before it reached the fields.

The next morning dawned clear and cool. We crawled
from the tunnel to find the village oddly smashed, some
houses untouched and whole sections of it gone. We set
about burying the dead.

1979 and 1993, the Afghan government lowered the age at which

Hedayat's family took us in. Their house was damaged, but it still stood. Hassan and Hedayat gathered up hundreds of pieces of sun-dried bricks, which were all that remained of our home, and quickly repaired the walls of our cousins' house. They made mortar of dust and water, straw and manure, using the brick pieces to build an extra room to accommodate us three girls and Ahmed. Hassan slept with Hedayat in the main room.

One of Hedayat's sisters, Fariel, had been injured, her leg torn badly. She was deaf from the blast, and lay on a cot in a fever. We took turns sitting with her, whisking the heat away from her in the afternoon with a Chinese silk fan, keeping the flies from her bandages, which soaked through with blood as soon as we changed them. We gave her water, dabbing it on her lips until she was able to swallow.

Watching our mother die had hardened Hassan. Something had turned in him that I knew would never turn back. He had been a gentle boy with a quick sense of humor, but now he stared straight ahead, spoke seldom, and never smiled.

I first understood that we were losing Hassan when Amina obeyed him without question. She brought him water before he asked. She was afraid—as I was—that he would leave, and she obeyed to keep him with us as long as possible.

But Hassan hardly seemed to notice. He seldom asked for anything. He spoke only in simple phrases, the minimum needed to convey what he meant. He and Hedayat worked side by side throughout the days. After the walls of Hedayat's house were repaired, they worked in the fields, which had been ruined in the bombing. Both families' winter stores of squash, carrots, potatoes, onions, and wheat were gone.

The grapes—those sweet, magical globes—escaped the notice of the helicopters, and we continued to pick them to buy wheat for the winter. That would leave us with little money for anything else. A few chickens and two goats had survived, so we would have eggs and milk, and many of the almond trees were left standing. We harvested apples and apricots to dry in the sun. Our other goats had died in the bombing, and Amina and I skinned them to make blankets: Winter was not far off, and our shawls had been destroyed, along with our other clothing and furnishings.

I began to wonder when our father would return. Men came and went from the village. Having heard of the attack, they brought their families things they had lost and could not afford to buy in the city market. But our father had been home only once since the war started last winter. I wondered if he was dead, too.

The weather was mild that autumn, fine for harvesting. Hassan planted a crop of winter wheat, in spite of knowing there was not enough time for it to ripen before the weather turned cold. We worked quietly, still stunned by the loss of our mother and all of our possessions. Our cousin Fariel began to mend, and we tried to hope.

Hedayat's mother reminded us that we were lucky. Some children in the village had lost their entire families and their houses, she said. Her words were meant to comfort us, but

to fifteen. In 1982, military training in the public schools because of them we mourned in silence, crying silently as we lay on our backs on the cot we shared, our tears pooling in our ears.

We still believed that Allah was with us, that He would not abandon unarmed children in the face of such brutality, and that the war against the infidels would end soon. But still our father did not come.

The older boys took turns, three at a time, herding the animals in the pale brown hills around the village and fields and keeping watch for the enemy's return. One day at noon, about a month after the attack that had nearly destroyed our village, the helicopter gunships returned. Hassan came running from the hillside where he'd been tending the goats.

"Run!" he shouted. "Quickly! To the tunnels! The Soviets are coming!" Everyone obeyed immediately. I was carrying water, and I dropped the pot, scooping up Ahmed and grabbing Farida's hand as I ran. My heart was in my mouth, and in my mind's eye I saw my mother turning for Ahmed's shawl, then whirling and lurching forward, her eyes staring in death.

Again we huddled in the chill damp of the irrigation tunnels. I sat the night without sleeping, one arm around Farida, the other around Ahmed, my back resting against the tunnel wall, my cheek against Ahmed's round, curly head. They nestled against me and slept soundly, for the night was oddly silent. No bombs thudded into the earth. The only sounds in the tunnel were the murmur of women praying softly, the rustle of clothing as people turned in their sleep, gentle snoring, and the occasional drip of water.

The silence was more ominous than the bombs. Had they landed their helicopters? Were they looking for us on foot? Would they shoot us all down where we sat in the tunnels?

At dawn Hassan and Hedayat and another boy crept from the tunnel to see whether it was safe for the rest of us to emerge into the day. They were gone a long time, and when they returned they told us we must remain where we were. The little ones cried because they were hungry, but we remained in the tunnel through the next day, when Hedayat and Hassan went out again. When they came back, they told us we could come back to the village.

The morning was bright and cool, and autumn smelled fresh and bitter in the air. There was another smell—of spoiled eggs, perhaps, but sweeter. Hassan told us the goats and sheep and chickens were gone.

"They were dead when we came out," he said, more words than he'd spoken in the weeks since our mother had died. "We found large cans—heavy white metal with silver knobs—four of them in the hills around the village. When we found the goats, they were dead, but they hadn't been shot. The flesh had already separated from their bones. There must have been a poison in the cans that corrupted the bodies, so that it was difficult to move them. We buried the cans with them."

From that time onward we lived with an even more terrible fear—that the Soviets would stop at nothing to kill us all.

it is estimated that there are ten to fifteen million land mines

When the helicopters raided a third time, they left behind a horror more terrifying than the poison in the metal cans. We emerged from the tunnels fearfully, but the village seemed unchanged. We saw nothing, heard nothing, and this made us even more apprehensive. Amina made us stay inside our room in our cousins' house the whole next day. Hassan and the older boys were in the hills, hidden under shawls the color of the dirt, keeping watch.

That afternoon a bang as loud as a gunshot echoed from the hills above the village. Farida cried, and we all had the same thought: Was Hassan safe? No one knew what the bang was, and we worried that the enemy was in the hills and would soon swarm down to the village and shoot us dead. That evening Hassan came back with Hedayat. We cried with relief when we saw them. Daoud, one of the other boys who kept watch in the hills, did not come home. Hassan and Hedayat went with Daoud's brother and his cousin to look for him.

The four returned carrying Daoud, his face white in the moonlight. His head rolled about on his neck as the boys hurried awkwardly down the path with him in their arms and into the village. Daoud's left leg dangled from just below the knee, and the foot was missing. Hedayat's mother and her sister, Daoud's aunt, cut off the rest of his leg that night with a butchering knife to save his life.

Daoud said he had stepped on something as he walked along the crest of a hill and the last thing he remembered was a loud bang like a rifle shot and pain shooting through his leg. In the days that followed two other boys were injured in a similar way. Hedayat and Hassan and the others searched the area and found several dozen plastic disks the size of a man's hand that looked like earth-colored butterflies with deadly bodies between the wings, each containing a small metal mechanism. The boys, using long, heavy poles, exploded all the ones they were able to find. The helicopters had scattered these tan butterflies on the ground so that the hills we loved—the hills that turned purple at dusk and shone like gold at dawn—would explode beneath our feet.

In the weeks that followed, the helicopters came three more times, dropping from their underbellies a form of death that was unspeakable. Scattered about the hillsides were toys, cameras, and watches—gifts that families in our village longed for but could never afford. Amina warned us to touch nothing on the ground. Every mother warned her children.

But one day, two boys slipped away when their mothers were not watching. They climbed up into the hills, avoiding the places where Hedayat and Hassan and the others stood guard. Mahsood, who was my age, picked up a wristwatch he found lying under a small bush. He reasoned that it could not have fallen from the sky and landed under a bush, and that it must be a real watch. The next instant the watch exploded, shattering his hands and putting out his eyes.

Even after what happened to Mahsood, other boys were tempted, and they, too, were scarred horribly.

One night I was awakened by a quiet stirring in the next room. Afraid that the Soviet soldiers would catch us sleeping

of the late 1990s, someone in the world was being injured, maimed, in our beds and shoot us, I got up without disturbing Amina, Farida, and Ahmed, and crept to the doorway, which was covered with a felt rug. I pulled the edge of the rug aside, and in the dim moonlight from the open doorway, I saw Hedayat and Hassan moving about. They both were dressed and were just rolling up the sides of their woolen hats and pulling them down to the tops of their ears.

I knew they were leaving. I stepped through the doorway and stood before them, but my throat was swollen shut with the threat of tears. Hassan took me gently by the shoulders.

"Go back to sleep," he whispered. "I will see you... soon." His voice faltered, and he hugged me quickly, his cheek silky against mine. I remembered the roughness of my father's chin as he'd hugged us each good-bye before leaving—also in the middle of the night. Hassan held the felt rug aside for me to go back to my bed. I turned and threw my arms around him, as if to keep him, pinning his arms to his sides. He pried me away and laid his hand against my face for a moment, then turned and was gone.

I did go back to bed and—believing Hassan's going was only a dream—I went back to sleep. That morning we awoke to the screams of Hedayat's mother.

"Hedayat!" she cried. "Where are you?" We were weary of screams by then, having heard so many cries of pain and terror. I stayed in bed, but Amina leapt up and ran with sleep in her eyes to see what the matter was. Hedayat's mother ran from the house screaming, "My son! Hedayat!"

or killed by a land mine every twenty-two seconds. About half of

When Amina returned, her face was a mask. She had known, as I had, that Hassan would go.

Word spread that many guns had come from America and Saudi Arabia, and that there were not enough men to take them up to fight the Soviets. Many of the older boys in our village—almost every male older than ten years—left in the following weeks to join the *mujahideen*.

That winter Amina, Farida, Ahmed, and I walked across the snowy hills to Pakistan, where the refugee camps were.

Amina went every day with our identification cards and collected our rations, coming back to report news of the fighting. The *mujahideen* claimed to be winning the war, but it was difficult for us to believe them. Still, we never gave up hope, because Amina said our father and Hassan depended on our believing in their holy war.

Hedayat came back once to tell us Hassan was well. He'd led a group of boys in an attack on a column of tanks in the Panjshir Valley to the north of Kabul. With rocks and bare fists they'd killed all of the soldiers as they emerged from their tanks, Hedayat said. Hassan was to be rewarded with guns and his own unit to command.

"When will he come to us?" Amina asked.

"If he's commanding, how can he leave?" Hedayat said.

Amina did not react in front of Hedayat, but that night I couldn't sleep, and I heard Amina crying next to me. I reached over and held her hand.

After a while Hedayat didn't come back to the camps either, and we never saw Hassan or our father again.

these victims were children. (8)

Sounds of Thunder

Joseph Bruchac

"Walk toward the sound of the guns."

Lewis Bowman looked to his right and to his left. None of the men, some of them as young as he was, had anything to say in response to the captain's order. What could they say? Even though that order made no sense—even a fifteen-year-old like him could see that—all of them were wearing the same uniform: Union blue. When you wore that uniform, you did whatever the men with stripes on their shoulders said, even when it meant you were about to march into a meat grinder.

This captain was a new one. He hadn't been in a battle yet, and he looked as if he was eager for it. Lewis wasn't quite sure what his name was. Either Sumber or Dumber. Probably the second one. "Most of 'em," Artis had said, "is eager for it till they get the first bullet in 'em."

Their last captain had died right in front of Lewis's eyes in the second battle at that little farm where the Rebs were hiding behind the rocks, not walking out in broad daylight like cows being driven to the slaughter. That captain, Evans was his name, had raised his sword and started to speak. Lewis remembered every word. "Boys of New York," Captain Evans had said, "let us show them what we are made of—"

Then the mortar shell that landed on his feet did a better job than his words of showing what he was made of—mostly blood.

Lewis looked behind him and caught a nod from Artis Cook. The same grim nod Artis had given him as they watched the men from the other company pour down the slope like ants streaming out a hill some farmer kicked while he was plowing. Just like those ants, the men of that company got stomped by the cannons and mortars and minié balls. *If we be ants,* Lewis thought, *them Rebs is hornets.*

That first assault was over quicker than a summer downpour, thunder and all. All that was left was not pools of water in the sun, but piles of dead and dying men, some crying out for their mothers with their last breaths. The firing had stopped as soon as the last of the men in Union blue went down. The Rebs were short of ammunition, like always. They made up for it by making every cannon shot and mortar shell and ball of lead count.

Lewis kept his eyes locked on the eyes of Artis Cook. He'd not met Artis more'n two weeks ago, but they had formed a bond. Not only were they the same age, but their brown faces showed that the two boys had more in common than a life spent in the sun. They were both Indians.

Lewis recalled how they met. At the bivouac outside of Gettysburg, he smelled something cooking from back in the brush. He looked around. No one else seemed to have caught that scent. Then he made as if to go and answer a call of nature. When no one was looking, he started to work his way back into the thick woods, moving so quiet that none of the other men in the company would have heard him. It was how he'd been taught to move by his father.

Quiet as he was, the one who'd been cooking had heard him. When Lewis entered the little clearing, he saw the fire, the rabbit on the spit, but no sign of the one who had caught it. Lewis understood. He raised his hands over his head. "You got me," he said in a soft voice. "Come on out, I'm a friend."

"Turn around," an equally soft voice answered.

Lewis had turned to look into the gun barrel and then the smiling eyes of a young man with long jet-black hair covered by a Union cap, a face round as a circle, and a nose that looked to have been broken more than its share of times.

Then Artis Cook lowered his gun. "Let's eat," he said.

From then on, wherever Lewis was, Artis was close behind. Artis had been separated from his own company—a good many of them Mohawk Indians like himself, volunteers from the St. Regis Reservation. In the last battle there had been such a scattering of men that new regiments and companies had to be put together like patchwork quilts from the remnants of torn clothing. Artis had ended up assigned to Lewis's squad, a private like himself. The first time they spoke to each other had been that day over the rabbit, but the two young men had been silently watching each other ever since Artis's arrival.

"You're Indian," Lewis said, over bites of rabbit leg.

Many hoped that participation in the war would persuade the

"Uh-huh."

"Mohawk, I'd bet," Lewis continued. It was already clear he'd have to carry most of the weight of words. It didn't make him uncomfortable. He was used to such conversations.

"Humh," Artis answered. "You?"

"Mostly," Lewis said. "We got some French, and some of us call ourselves that, just to avoid trouble, you know? I was born up to St. Francis, but my family has been coming down to Saratoga for years. That's where I joined up."

"Abenaki?" Artis said, raising an eyebrow.

"That's right," Lewis said. "I be St. Francis Abenaki."

Artis laughed. "Then you should not of et that rabbit." He slapped the trunk of the pine tree next to him. "You should have et this, you Adirondack!"

It was the longest statement yet, the most words Lewis would ever hear at one time from his new friend. But it made him angry. Adirondack! That was the word the Iroquois used for his people, who sometimes used the inner bark of pines for food. Adirondack meant his people were porcupines, foolish bark-eaters.

Lewis narrowed his eyes. "Well, you know where you got your name, don't you, Mohawk? We give it to you. Maguak! That means 'coward' in my language."

Artis didn't answer with words. In one jump he was over the fire and the two of them were wrestling in the dirt. It ended with Artis sitting on top of Lewis's chest. One of Lewis's elbows had caught Artis in the nose, and blood was dripping from it, but he paid no attention to it.

government to change its policies toward Native Americans and

A rumble of thunder—real thunder, not distant cannon—came from the west.

Artis nodded down at Lewis.

"Grandfathers, we call them," Lewis said from his back. A stick was poking into his shoulder blade.

"Uh-huh," Artis said. He stood, stretched out a hand, and helped Lewis to his feet. Then he reached down to a pouch hung from his side. Some sort of medicine bag? Lewis thought. Artis held the pouch up and shook it so that it made a rattling sound.

"Marbles," he said. "Want to play?"

Lewis grinned. "For certain sure!" he said.

Men they might be in battle, carrying rifles and bayonets, but they were also still boys. Lewis pulled out the gray handkerchief that held his own small store of clay marbles. They made a circle in the dry earth and played until the light began to fail and the call back to camp sounded. From then on, whenever there were a few hours of quiet, that was what they did. They played. Sometimes it was mumblety-peg with their pocketknives, but most often it was marbles. Whether by luck or skill, neither of them ever won all of the other's, though every marble changed hands a dozen times.

Artis proved a good friend in more ways than one. Though others might go to bed hungry, Artis was not one of them. Somehow he always managed to find food. If it wasn't a rabbit or a squirrel, it was berries or roots. It seemed to Lewis that if there was ever more than a moment's pause in the line of march, Artis would have a fire started and be

put an end to the forced removal of tribes from their ancestral cooking something over it. Whatever he cooked or gathered, half of it was always for Lewis.

Today, there was no time for cooking. Men were waiting on the other side of that pasture to kill them. The field looked peaceful enough. Where it hadn't yet been trampled down by the feet of charging men, the hay was waving in the summer wind.

It is just right for cutting, Lewis thought. But the only thing that will be mowed here today is men.

Artis put his hand on Lewis's shoulder. "Listen," he whispered.

Lewis listened. Artis had heard it before him. A roll of thunder sounded off to the west. A storm was on its way, though it would, for certain sure, arrive after the storm of lead and fire.

"Grandfathers watch over you," Artis said. The way he said it made Lewis feel calm. He and Artis had talked about thunder. Heno was what Mohawks called the thunder beings, the grandfathers. His own Abenaki people called them Bedagiak. The thunder beings were ancient grandfathers who cared for the people. When they struck the earth with their arrows of lightning, they were trying to destroy bad things. Then they brought the rain to cleanse the earth. No matter where you went, they were there in the sky above you, even when you were so far away from home. At least that was what Lewis's father had told him once. He hoped it was true.

A bugle sounded. The new captain stepped forward and

raised his sword. There was the crumping sound of a mortar shell being fired from a rebel battery. Both Artis and Lewis took a step backward. But the shell landed well in front of them. The captain pointed with his sword.

"That way, men," the captain said. "To the sound of the guns."

Then they were all moving, walking one foot after another. The thudding and thumping of the cannons and mortars was starting, not just from before but also from behind as their own artillerymen opened fire. There was fire and smoke in front of them. It made Lewis think of the hell that Father Andre up at Odanak had preached about. He didn't know if he was on his way to Father Andre's hell, but he was certain sure heading into this one on earth.

They were too far away to hit anyone with their rifles yet, and they were still walking. Suddenly there was a great explosion right next to them. Men fell around Lewis as dirt and stones went spinning past his face. His cheeks were both wet. When he reached up to wipe them clean, his hand came down all red. He didn't know if it was his own blood.

Someone pulled on his sleeve. He looked over. It was Artis. He had his mouth open and was shouting something. Lewis couldn't make it out. Then he realized that he was deaf, deaf from the cannonball that had struck so close. Artis jerked his sleeve again and there was a popping in Lewis's ears. He could hear again.

"The hell with walking," Artis was yelling. "Run!"

Then they began to run, not away from the battle but

change in policy occurred. While freed slaves were granted

toward the enemy line. If they ran, there might be less chance of getting shot. If they got close enough, they could fire their guns with at least the chance of hitting something.

A gray shape like a ghost rose up out of the smoke, thrusting a bayonet at the end of a rifle. It tore the shoulder of Lewis's coat before Artis leaped in and knocked the Confederate soldier aside with his shoulder. The man fell down as they ran on.

They ran and ran. They ran through clouds of smoke, past men who lay on the ground crying out for help, past the broken branches of trees. They ran through a sudden swirling shower of maple leaves that spun down around them as a nearby blast stripped a tree at the field edge. Lewis felt as if his lungs were on fire. Then he noticed that things were quieter. The fighting was behind him.

"Artis," Lewis said, "we got through."

No one answered. Lewis looked around. He was alone: Artis had disappeared.

He looked ahead. There, through the smoke, he could make out something. A tree had fallen down, knocked over by a cannon blast. It was a place where he could take shelter and figure out what to do next. Lewis began to walk toward it, his breath gradually slowing.

Sudden as a squirrel, someone in gray popped up from behind the tree and fired. The rebel soldier was no more than ten paces away, but he missed. The minié ball passed by Lewis's face with an angry sizzling sound. Lewis raised his own rifle to his shoulder to fire. He knew that he would not miss.

Then he saw the frightened face of the person who'd shot at him. The Reb was a boy younger than him, so young he'd barely been able to lift that long old rifle. Lewis lowered his gun and raised a hand. He pushed it forward and nodded.

"Thank ye," the boy whispered. He turned and ran.

Lewis watched him go. The boy's tattered gray uniform was so big for him that he'd rolled the legs of the pants up to his knees and the buttonless coat flapped on him like a scarecrow's shirt caught in the wind. Lewis shook his head as he stepped forward and placed his hand on the tree trunk. He was only fifteen, but he'd seen enough war already for a man three times his age.

All of a sudden, the whole world turned upside down. Everything got blacker than the darkest midnight and then even the blackness was gone.

Lewis tried to open his eyes. He couldn't. They were glued shut. He went to raise his right arm to wipe his face clean. The arm wouldn't move and for a moment he wondered if it was still there or blown clean off. He tried again, and he could feel his arm now. As he strained to move it, fiery pain swept over him, and he lost consciousness. Perhaps it was only for a moment. Perhaps it was for a day. He had no way to tell.

When he came to, he heard a strange rasping sound. Someone was breathing near him, ragged painful breaths. He realized it was himself he was hearing. This time he didn't try to move the right arm that was pinned beneath him. Slowly, carefully, he attempted to flex the fingers on the left hand he felt resting on his chest. They moved! A great wave of excitement swept over him. An inch at a time he walked his left hand up toward his face. Something was crusted over his eyes. He scraped away the mud that had dried there. Tears flowed, washing his eyes clean, and he could see. The tree he had been touching still lay there next to him. Its bark was torn now by the second cannon blast that had struck so close to him.

Lewis was half in a sitting position, and, though he couldn't seem to get up, he could move his head. He looked down. One, two. His legs were both still there. They were not in one of those baskets of arms and legs outside the surgeons' tents. One of his boots had been knocked off. There were his toes. He tried to wiggle them. All five moved.

"Hurrah," he said in a weak voice. Whatever had been done to him, whatever damage he'd suffered, was mostly inside him and in his right arm, it seemed. Then the thought of his marbles came to him. Had he lost them? He slid his left arm back down along his side. His heart leaped when his fingers found the cotton pouch still tied to his belt and the hard, round shapes of the marbles. Though it hurt his face to do so, he couldn't help but smile.

But he was so weak, so thirsty. "I need help," he said in a voice he knew was too small to hear even if someone had been near. He tried to pull himself up with his left arm, but the pain from his right shoulder and arm drove through him like a bayonet, and he blacked out again.

When he woke again, his throat was dry. It was so dry that he felt as if he couldn't breathe. "Grandfathers," he croaked.

A distant rumble sounded in answer. Then the thunder sounded again much closer. The next flash of the lightning was no more than fifty yards away, and it shook the earth. But Lewis was not afraid. He could hear the rain walking across the dry earth toward him. He leaned back his head and opened his mouth as the rain fell, a steady, heavy rain. It wet his face, washing away the mud and blood of battle, quenching his thirst.

"Bedagiak," Lewis Bowman whispered, "I thank you for my life."

He reached out his good left hand and tore a piece of the pale, starchy inner bark from the pine tree next to him. As he placed it into his mouth, he thought for a moment about what Artis would say when he found him. Then he smiled and began to chew.

Witness

Jennifer Armstrong

This was how we got the news: One of the deacons from our church, Mr. Remington, came to our house to tell us. Dad and I were finishing dinner. It was only about five-thirty, still plenty of light, and you could hear lawn mowers and someone in the neighborhood had started a charcoal fire; you could smell the lighter fluid. Someone was going to have a cookout, but we were already finishing our dinner. I guess I already said that, but I want to get all the details correct. Our dinner was frozen lasagna that I put in the oven at 350 degrees for an hour, according to the package directions, and a salad that I made from a prewashed mixture of lettuce from the Price Chopper and low-cal ranch dressing. Also garlic bread. I had milk; Dad had a beer. It was Miller Lite. These details are important. A lot of times you don't notice things, and then you find out later you should have. It was five-thirty. It was still light.

Take, for example, those brain teasers where someone keeps saying how many people got off the bus and then on the bus, and you're so busy keeping track of how many people there are, doing the math in your head, all the addition and subtraction and being sure you're too smart to be stumped by a dumb riddle like this, that you don't realize you're being tricked, that the real question is how many stops did the bus make. A lot of times you're paying attention to something that you think is going to be important, and then it turns out that you were paying attention to the totally wrong things. You totally missed it.

Mr. Remington is one of the deacons at our church, as I said. He is a dentist, although not my dentist. I know his first name is John, and his wife's first name is Susan. Or Suzanne—I'm not positive which. They live in a white house with green shutters on Caroline Street, and at Halloween every year they give out toothbrushes, not candy. They have a handicapped kid who goes to a special school. His name is Johnny. When Mr. Remington came to the kitchen door, he was wearing khaki pants and a blue shirt, no tie, and he said through the screen door, "Sorry for interrupting your dinner," and my dad said we were just finishing and took his napkin out from being tucked in at the neck. Mr. Remington looked at me and then at my dad and said, "Can I talk to you outside, Rich?" It was five-thirty. Actually, to be precise, it was five-thirty-five. I looked at the clock on the oven when Mr. Remington said that to my dad.

I began clearing the dishes. Our dishes are white with a design of red checks around the edge and cherries in the middle, three cherries. Life is a bowl of cherries, my mom always said when she put out my cereal bowl at breakfast time. But you have to understand that she always said it as if life was a bowl of sour cherries, and I got so sick of her saying that every morning, as if she'd never said it before, that I had to find a way of blocking out her voice without seeming to, like hunching my shoulders to cover my ears, or coughing real loud so I couldn't hear—anything.

There's a window over the sink. I started running water over the dishes and looked out the window. The sky was blue, blue jay blue, really intense, almost neon, and the sun had that special kind of sideways look to it when there's still plenty of daylight left but you know it's getting to be late late afternoon, evening really, and Mr. Remington's and Dad's shadows were walking giant steps beside them down the driveway. Mr. Remington had his hand on Dad's shoulder. He wore a gold pinky ring with a red stone. Dad put one hand over his eyes and stopped walking, and Mr. Remington reached out as if afraid my dad would fall. Two cars drove by, a green minivan and a blue minivan. Mr. Remington's car was parked at the end of our driveway. The license plate was OCAV-T; I remember that because he's a dentist. I always notice these things now.

When you're little, you notice kid things. Things that are at your eye level. Like how, when you go into the bank with your mother, and she's standing at the counter that has a thick piece of glass on it, and you can look into the edge of the glass and inside are lines and lines of green that go on forever, like a ladder inside the thick pane of glass that has no bottom and no top and no edges, and even though your mother is arguing with someone about a country and a war you don't know where it is, you're imagining getting inside

Nicaragua. Approximately four thousand Americans traveled

the glass to climb that ladder. If your mother argues all the time about things in other countries and people she isn't even related to, that's what you notice, how you could get inside the glass and climb the ladder. You could go up or down, it doesn't matter which.

Once, when I was in the bank with my mother, and I was looking inside the edge of the glass and she was arguing with someone, she left me there. She walked right out of the door of the bank and crossed Broadway without even looking. Cars honked at her and screeched their brakes, and then she whipped around right in the middle of the street and strode back into the bank to take my hand. I wanted to stay looking inside the edge of the glass. I was crying because I wanted to climb the ladder.

But that's stupid stuff, kid stuff. It doesn't mean anything. Forget it.

These are the kinds of things you notice when you're older: You notice what other kids your age wear and how they walk. You notice if your teacher has the right kind of shoes, and sometimes it makes a difference as to whether or not you believe he's a fair grader. You notice that your mother always embarrasses you by talking too emotionally about genocide and ethnic cleansing and land mines and the United Nations, and you notice if other people are looking at you when you're with her and she's not talking about regular things like the school board elections or the weather. You wonder why, if your mom loves you the way moms are sup-posed to, she would do this to you.

When Mom announced at dinner she was going to be a Witness for Life in Bosnia with some other people from our church, my father threw his napkin down and left the room, and it was really awful because my friend Raelynne was over to do homework with me and my mother cursed, actually said the F-word. I couldn't even really listen to her explain how the church was sending volunteer witnesses to war zones to try to prevent war crimes and atrocities by just being there and keeping the governments on their toes because they were watching, being witnesses. All the time she was talking, I was looking at Raelynne sideways and wondering what she thought. So because of that, because of wondering about Raelynne, I didn't notice the other things I should have noticed while Mom was talking.

I didn't notice these other things until Mr. Remington came to our house. But this was how I started noticing: I was sitting at the table with Dad, finishing my salad, and I looked up, and through the screen door I saw Mr. Remington coming up the brick walkway in his khaki pants and his blue shirt, and I knew there were not many reasons for a church deacon going to a neighbor's house unannounced right at dinnertime, even though it was still early, and I heard a lawn mower start up.

So I was already studying the details when he said, "Can I talk to you outside, Rich?" and that's how I know it was five-thirty-five, and that there were things that had mattered more to my mother than her own daughter did. That was a detail I had never really noticed before—that sometimes

everything isn't about you, and you better start paying attention, because maybe if I'd been a better witness, I could've
stopped this from happening.

War Is Swell

David Lubar

As the second burst of machine-gun fire tore the air with its deadly rhythm, Jorgi clutched his stomach and fell to the floor, curling his body into a tight ball around the pain that exploded through his gut.

He called to his little sister, who was sprawled on her back just beyond his reach, "Katya?"

"It hurts," she said, her words half smothered by the rumble of an exploding mortar shell.

"We didn't know," he said. A shower of plaster fell from the ceiling. Jorgi closed his eyes and fought against the panic that came whenever the earth shook, but this tremor was brief and the building was sturdy.

"We were pigs," Katya said.

"Yes, pigs," Jorgi agreed. "I never guessed it could hurt so much." He rose to his knees, then gave up and dropped back to the floor. It was too soon to try to stand. Despite the pain, he had to smile. He'd known hunger all his life. It was a familiar pain, made worse these past few weeks when nobody had food to spare. Who would have thought there was far worse pain in eating too much?

"Let's not be pigs next time," Katya said.

"Just be happy we're here," Jorgi said. He couldn't believe their luck. They'd been alone on the street right before sunrise when Abnar, the baker, fled. Abnar, who had never willingly given either of them so much as a small crust, left the village with his cart, his horse, and his family. He'd also left one important thing behind—an unlocked door. Inside, they found a treasure of bread, cookies, and two wedding cakes.

Ten minutes after they'd entered the bakery, Jorgi thought he'd never need to eat again. The crumbs of his victims littered the floor. A trail of ants had already joined the feast, streaming out from a large gap where the floorboards met the wall. As he watched them swarm over a piece of fallen cake, Jorgi wondered whether ants ever got stomach aches.

Katya stood and walked to the table that held the pair of wedding cakes. With a grunt, she tried to move the smaller one, but even that was too heavy for her.

"What are you doing?" Jorgi asked.

"I want to make them pretty again," she said.

"Let me help." Jorgi forced himself to his feet. He turned the cakes so the ruined parts faced the wall. "There. Just the way we found them." He didn't feel guilty about scooping handfuls from both cakes. The brides had left three days ago, with the growing stream of people who'd headed for the western border since the fighting reached the village. The grooms had joined the fighting. The cakes were already growing dry, the icing stiff. There would be no weddings.

For months, Jorgi had sensed rising tension in the voices

fought around the world, most in poor countries. In the past of the old men who sat all day outside the café. They drank glasses of hot tea, passed around tattered newspapers, and talked in angry bursts about who was to blame for all the trouble. They'd seemed so concerned with the battle reports that none of them even bothered to chase Jorgi off with stones and curses the way they usually did.

The bakery shook as another mortar shell turned the empty stable across the street into a pile of splinters. A mountain of hay drifted down, lagging behind the rest of the debris as if it were eager to play in the spring breeze. Early-morning rays of sunlight danced among the pieces.

"It's raining gold," Katya said, staring out the window.

"Let's go," Jorgi said. He filled a box with bread, picking the freshest loaves he could find.

Katya grabbed another box, which she loaded with cookies. "Back home?" she asked.

"No." Jorgi shook his head. Their home, an abandoned truck at the end of an alley three blocks away, was too close to the path of the mortars. They needed to find a new place. Jorgi liked the river. At night, the peaceful murmur of the water was better than any music. But some of the older men lived there—the ones who were too poor to spend their days at the café. Those men shouted at him and stole his food—food he had worked so hard to find for himself and Katya. No, not the river. They could go to the hills. Jorgi knew which plants were safe to eat. But they'd have to be careful to avoid the soldiers, who swarmed the hills like ants. Like ants on a cake....

decade alone, because of war, two million children were killed,

"I know," Jorgi said, amazed that such a perfect idea had taken so long to come to him. "Abnar's house."

"Yes," Katya said. Her leap of excitement bounced several small cookies from the box. "A bed," she said. "I'll bet there's a bed to sleep on. And maybe even a pillow."

"We'll see," Jorgi said. He didn't want her to hope for too much. Katya was such a dreamer. To her, the old truck where they usually slept was a castle one day and a sailing ship the next. Flat stones turned into plates and saucers when she served feasts to her make-believe friends. At least the baker's house, at the top of a small hill to the east, was far from the center of the village, out of mortar range for the moment. Most of the shelling appeared to be aimed at the small cluster of government buildings that lined the main road near the larger shops—though, from what Jorgi had seen, nobody seemed to be able to aim anything very well.

"Listen," Katya said as they left the bakery and climbed over the splintered boards that had once been a stable wall. "No more bombs."

"They haven't stopped," Jorgi said. "I'll bet there'll be another one before I can count to ten." He started counting, quickly at first, but then stretching out each number longer than the one before. When he reached nine, he used every bit of air in his lungs to keep the sound alive. Finally, he gave up, took a deep breath, and said, "Ten."

Far behind them, a blast blew another hole in the street. Jorgi gritted his teeth as a jolt passed through the ground. To his left, near the butcher's shop, a young tree trembled, its leaves shivering in the sudden wind. A moment later, cobblestones rained down in the distance with the sound of galloping horses.

"Let me try," Katya said. "I know my numbers." She started counting. A mortar shell fell when she reached seven. As she hunched over against the shock wave, she spat out the rest, "Eightnineten. I did it!"

"You sure did," Jorgi said, smiling at his sister. He stepped around a broken bicycle that had been abandoned in the road. "You're very clever, Katya." It was true. He remembered the time he'd had the fever. Katya had taken care of him for three days, cooling his head with water from the river and grinding food into a paste he could swallow past his swollen throat. She was more than just clever—she was brave.

"Go on. It's your turn," she said as they left the main road for the narrower path that led up the hill.

Jorgi reached ten without an explosion.

"My turn," Katya said. A mortar shell blew up far to their left while she counted. "That's two for me."

They played the game all the way to the baker's house, which sat in the center of a large yard, surrounded by a whitewashed wall. The gate was open.

"Wait here," Jorgi said after they walked down the brick pathway and stepped inside the front entrance. He needed to make sure everything was safe. As he dashed from room to room, he saw no sign of damage. No ceilings ready to crumble, no walls ready to topple like that dreadful moment—the day

when the earth shook and the walls crushed his world, burying their parents, leaving him and Katya alone.

The memory of the earthquake was barely more than a
dream now. How long? Three years? Four? What was the difference? Somehow, they'd survived, day by day. Always hungry,
always cold in the winter, hot in the summer. But alive. They'd
found their way to this village, but never found a home, never
found people who could afford to offer them more than a brief
moment of kindness or a scrap of food.

"There's not one bed," Jorgi told Katya when he returned
to her.

"No?" she asked, her face growing dark with disappoint-
ment.

"No. Not one. There are five!" he shouted, lifting his sister by her waist and spinning around.

"Can I pick first?" she asked when he put her down.

"Of course."

The mortars stopped for a while, as did most of the
gunfire. They slept well that night, and ate well again in the
morning.

In the afternoon, they sat on the warm red-tile roof of the
house, a terrifying and exhilarating three stories above the
ground, and watched as a group of men dug holes in the north
road and planted land mines. They made a game of guessing
where the men would dig next—left, right, or center. Katya
was good at the game, which made Jorgi proud. "You're very
smart, little sister," he told her.

The next morning, they discovered that the butcher had

also fled, leaving behind unbelievable riches. Jorgi cooked thick lamb steaks in the baker's kitchen, frying them in a pan with onions he'd found in the cellar. A sweet, satisfying aroma filled the air as the meat sizzled. They'd made three trips to the butcher's, bringing home sausages, too. The hard, dried ones with the wonderfully spicy flavor—the kind that would keep well in the coming heat of summer.

"Real plates," Katya said as she set the table. She rubbed her hand carefully across the blue flowers painted on the gleaming white china, then refolded the linen napkins until they were perfectly arranged.

They ate with heavy knives and forks of silver and drank their water from crystal goblets. Katya, giggling, shouted orders to the servants. Jorgi played along, unwilling to do anything that might break the spell for her.

That evening, they watched a different group of men dig up the mines. Jorgi kept count, and gave Katya a cookie for every fifth mine. It wasn't as much fun as the guessing game, but he still enjoyed the look on her face each time he got close to the magic number.

After sunset the airplanes came.

"It's beautiful," Katya said, holding her brother's hand as they stood on the balcony of the large bedroom, watching the dazzling flashes that bloomed like giant sunflowers wherever bombs struck the ground. She pointed at the brilliant streaks of light that danced from the earth toward the heavens.

"Those are called *tracers*," Jorgi explained. He loved to show her the things he'd learned from listening to the men.

injured in conflicts are civilians, mostly children and their

"They let the gunners know where their bullets are going so they can shoot the planes."

"Who's flying the planes?" Katya asked.

Jorgi shrugged. "I'm not sure." He knew that the soldiers attacking the village were enemies. The planes seemed to be bombing the enemy soldiers, so the planes must be friends. But sometimes the bombs hit the village, too. So maybe they weren't friends. Or at least not good friends. Right now, it really didn't matter, as long as none of the bombs hit the baker's house.

A plane exploded, turning the sky from deep black to red for a blinding instant. A lazy boom reached their ears several seconds later. "We used to have a festival," Jorgi said. Another faint memory. "This is like—" He stopped to find the word. "Fireworks!"

"I wish I could go to a festival," Katya said.

"You will, someday," Jorgi told her. "I promise. Not now. But when the war is over."

Katya gasped. "When the war is over?" Her hand slipped limply from Jorgi's grasp.

"Yes, when the war is over." It was a phrase he'd heard many times from the lips of nearly everyone in the village. *When the war is over* ... It was always followed by a plan or a dream or a hope. He watched as his sister turned and stared across the room at the plump feather bed with three pillows, each as soft as a baby rabbit.

Katya crossed to the foot of the bed and stood by the box of cookies for a moment. She stroked the bright quilt that was draped over the mattress, then returned to the window. She glanced toward the sky as the glow of a nearby explosion—a direct hit on an ammunition stockpile—highlighted her face.

Jorgi felt her tears burn small holes in his heart. Katya never cried. Not when she'd fallen and cut her knee so badly it had bled all day and half the night. Not when they'd gone nearly a week without food. Not even when she asked him about their parents. Now she wept as if she'd just lost all her dreams.

"Katya, don't cry," Jorgi said, trying to comfort his sister. As he looked around the room, he understood. In peacetime, they'd slept in a truck and eaten scraps. That was the only life Katya knew. Until the fighting started. When the war came, it brought them food, soft beds, fireworks, and games.

When the war is over . . . He thought of the way people said those words. It was with the same voice that said, *One day, when I'm rich,* or *If I were in charge,* or a thousand other impossible hopes.

Jorgi put his arm around Katya's thin shoulders. "It was a silly thing for me to say. A joke. That's all. A stupid joke. The war will never end."

"Promise?" she asked, huddling close to her brother.

Jorgi nodded. "I promise." In the sky, an anti-aircraft shell exploded like a bright star. Not the first star of the night, but maybe still good enough. "The war will never end," he told Katya, making a promise, making a wish.

Hope

Gloria D. Miklowitz

The old ship, *Palestine Hope,* creaked and groaned as it rode the waves like a tired horse. Hans sat on the dirty floor in the hold beside Sonya. Around him lay other children, curled up like worms. He had grown used to the smell of puke and human waste and ached to stretch, to walk on the open deck, smell the fresh air. But the deck above was just as crowded, with its teeming horde of war survivors, mostly Jews from all over Europe. And he did not want to leave Sonya.

"Sonya! Speak to me, please!" he begged. "Don't be afraid. I'll protect you!"

Hans touched the limp hand of the pale, skeletal girl on the ground beside him, but she flinched and drew back. Her eyes flickered from emptiness to terror. In the weeks he had been in the special camp, where the survivors were gathered until they could be placed elsewhere, he had met many others like Sonya. Some cried or screamed at night, remembering Bergen-Belsen, or Auschwitz, or any of the other concentration camps they had miraculously survived. But Sonya never uttered a sound.

He didn't know what drew him to the girl, what made

One and a half million children were killed during the Holocaust.

him watch over her. Maybe it was that she resembled the sister he only vaguely remembered. The sister who had loved and protected him as a child. Miriam had been blond, like Sonya, about ten years old, as Sonya was, only his sister had been rosy-cheeked and plump, always chattering and singing. That was a long time ago, seven years, before the war started, when he was only five. Much of that past was dim now except for one memory. It was the day he'd been sent to live with a Christian family, away from his own Jewish home in Germany. "I don't want to go!" he had sobbed, clinging to his mother.

"Big boys don't cry," his father replied, with tears in his eyes. "We will join you soon, my son. Miriam, too. As soon as it can be arranged."

But they hadn't. They'd been picked up by the Nazis soon after he had gone to live on the farm in Denmark. When he tried to find them after the war, the refugee agency said they had died in Auschwitz.

And now Hans sat beside Sonya in the dark hold of this old ship, on the way to Palestine—the land of milk and honey, of sunshine and hope. He spoke to her often, in German, her native language, never knowing if she heard or understood.

He folded his jacket and slid it under Sonya's head, then squeezed in to lie beside her. It was comforting to hear her steady breathing, almost like being close to Mama again.

"When we get to Palestine, I will see that we stay together," he whispered, thinking that she would be his sister

Few survived the concentration camps. When the camps were

now. "Maybe they'll send us to a farm, maybe where they grow oranges. It will be good. No barbed wire around us. No soldiers with guns. You will forget and grow healthy and strong."

Sonya whimpered. Nearby a small child called for water. Hans had taken over the role of nurse for the children because he was twelve and stronger, having lived on a farm during the war. He rose and climbed over the listless bodies to the water bucket. He filled a ladle and carried it back to the child, holding one hand under it to catch the precious drips, which he licked from his palm. Then he returned to Sonya.

As he thought about yesterday, a scared churning began in his stomach. The captain had announced that they would soon be within sight of Palestine. The news brought a cheer from the passengers, and someone began singing *"Hatikvah."* But then the captain added that British warships were following them. The Arabs did not want more Jews in Palestine, and the British, needing Arab oil, kept the Jews out. If the captain tried to take their ship, the *Palestine Hope,* to land, British soldiers would board her. They would arrest the captain and crew. All passengers would be forced off the ship and sent to the island of Cyprus.

Another concentration camp, Hans thought bitterly. They said over twenty-five thousand Jewish war survivors were there already, waiting for entry permits into Palestine. They were surrounded by two walls of barbed wire, living in tents under a broiling sun, with little water to drink. Dry winds whipped up the sand until one could hardly breathe,

liberated, there were about one thousand child survivors in

he'd been told. Those many thousands were joined each week by more survivors trying to get into Palestine. If he and Sonya were caught and sent to Cyprus, they might have to wait years for permits to enter the country.

There had been talk among the children in the hold after the captain's announcement. "I would rather die than go to another camp," a boy from Poland said in Yiddish. "I will jump into the sea and swim to Palestine!" a German girl said. "My uncle is in Haifa. He is my only family left!"

Hans listened, watching Sonya. Though her eyes darted from face to face as if she were listening, they revealed nothing. How could he reach her, give her hope? Did she think they would all be herded into camps again, like she had been in Germany?

The children had talked for hours. "We should fight the British if we want to survive," Hans argued. "No more letting others decide what to do with us! If I ever get to Palestine, I will become a soldier!"

Now a commotion above brought him to his feet. There were screams and shouts, and people scurried down the ladders into the already crowded hold. Suddenly, the ship shuddered and lurched. Hans felt as if all the blood had drained from his body. "Mama!" he whispered.

What happened? Had the ship struck something? Did a mine explode beneath them? Would the *Palestine Hope* go down now they were so close to freedom?

The captain's voice boomed from the loudspeaker. "Passengers of the *Palestine Hope*! We have been rammed by a British ship. Please remain calm. The damage is not serious. We are determined to bring you safely to Palestine, and nothing will stop us."

Nothing? The British had destroyers and weapons— though they dared not fire at a ship filled with remnants of the death camps. But they could surround the *Palestine Hope* and force it to shore as they had forced other ships trying to break the blockade. Then they'd be transferred to Cyprus.

"Come!" Hans ordered Sonya. He motioned to the other children. "All of you, come with me! If the ship sinks, it will be better to be on deck, where we can get into lifeboats." He grabbed Sonya's hand and drew her to the ladder. She floated behind him, as light as a ghost, up the stairs to the deck. He squeezed between others, pressing Sonya forward, to peer over the rails, out to sea.

"There!" he pointed. Palestine's coastline was so near he could almost smell the growing things. But—so far. It seemed impossible they would ever reach it. The ship that had rammed them played floodlights over them, lights so bright that he had to shield his eyes. Their ship bobbed in the water, surrounded, its engines silent. The British would never let them into Palestine.

About three in the morning, the engines started up again, and the *Palestine Hope* began moving, away from the coast. Where were they going? Please, God, no. Not back to the French port from where they'd come! Not back to Germany and the detention camps! Hans swallowed the hard lump in his throat and wiped at the tears stinging his

Ravensbruck, fourteen hundred in Dachau, and one hundred in

eyes. All the promises he had made to Sonya. Such foolish dreams—to think he could make them come true.

He stood at the rail, unable to bring himself to return to the hot, crowded hold below. Around him, people sobbed, prayed, stared hopelessly out to sea. It was dark now. They were probably at least three miles from shore, and the fog had moved in, almost hiding the British ships trailing them. "I tried, Sonya. I'm sorry," he said softly. "I really hoped we'd get there...."

And then it seemed the ship engines sounded louder, and the *Palestine Hope* picked up speed. Was he imagining this? The captain was putting greater distance between his ship and the British. Why? Was he trying to outrun the enemy? Suddenly, the *Palestine Hope* veered sharply left. Cries of fear filled the air. They were heading straight to shore. Hans gripped the handrails, his heart racing. Through the mist he saw lights on the beach—bonfires?

"*Palestine Hope!*" came the harsh voice from the closest British ship. "Reverse direction at once! This is an order! I warn you: Turn back to the course agreed upon, or we will fire!"

"He's taking us in!" Hans cried, his voice husky with wonder and emotion. "Those British ships are too big to come closer! We're going to land in Palestine!" Sonya's hand tightened in his.

A loud horn sounded, waking those who slept, and the captain's voice boomed out. "Passengers! Prepare to disembark! I am beaching this ship and we must evacuate quickly. Haganah agents are on shore to help."

Explosions sounded in the distance. Bright fires flared.

"Do not fear," the captain added. "The explosions you hear were set to divert British troops from rescue operations. But they cannot be fooled for long. Prepare to disembark!"

The *Palestine Hope* raced toward shore, the upper deck dense with men, women, and children, babbling in many languages, straining to see through the mist. Suddenly, close to shore, the ship slowed, then stopped abruptly, caught on a sandbar. Passengers cried out in terror. Hans gripped Sonya's arm.

Crew members dropped rope ladders from the sloping sides. Old and young pushed and shoved, chafing to be off the ship, down the ladders, to find their footing and slog through the low surf to land.

Hans helped Sonya into the water. She shivered at the sudden cold. "Soon you'll be warm," he said, pulling her with him. "Hurry!" He glanced back. The British ships could not chase closer because of the shallow depths.

The *Palestine Hope*'s passengers swarmed around them— crying, groaning, frantically moving toward shore. A wave splashed over them, and Sonya fell. Hans lifted her to his shoulder and stumbled on, panting and crying.

"Here! I'll take her!" a Haganah soldier said, wading into the surf to help. She reached for Sonya, carried her to the shore. "*Shalom,*" the soldier greeted them. "Welcome to Palestine." And then, "Hurry!" Dripping wet, Hans ran with Sonya up a path to waiting trucks. As each truck filled with children and adults from the *Palestine Hope,* it roared off into the dark night.

"We're here, Sonya. We're in Palestine! Can you believe it?" Hans exclaimed joyfully as they bumped over dirt roads. "Speak to me! Please! Let me know you understand!"

In the darkness, he could not see if his words reached her, but after a time she touched his arm, something she had never done. And with her face raised, she sniffed the air and said, "Oranges?"

Authors' Notes

Jennifer Armstrong:

"I have written about teens and war in a novel, *The Dreams of Mairhe Mehan*, and in a collaborative book, *In My Hands: Memories of a Holocaust Rescuer*. The juxtaposition of youth and war haunts me. They say war isn't an appropriate subject for young people, and you know what? I agree. But war doesn't care. That's why I decided to put this book together."

Jennifer Armstrong is the author of more than fifty books for children and young adults, both fiction and nonfiction. She lives in Saratoga Springs, New York, where she is always at work on another book.

Ibtisam Barakat:

"I am from Palestine, an Arab nation in the Middle East. In 1967, Israel launched a preemptive attack on its Arab neighbors. My story takes place on the second day of that war, known as the Six-Day War. My family lived in a town called Ramallah, and when the war started, we fled to Jordan. When we returned under the protection of the Red Cross, among a minority of families that returned, we lived under

Israeli military occupation. The violence in the Middle East continues today, and I believe that a chronic imbalance in how the story of Palestine is told contributes to the endless killing."

Ibtisam Barakat now lives in Missouri, where she is working on a memoir of the war.

Joseph Bruchac:

"My Abenaki great-grandfather, Lewis Bowman, was a veteran of the American Civil War, and this story draws on family traditions about my great-grandfather's actual experiences in a New York regiment."

Joseph Bruchac is a writer and storyteller whose work often reflects his Abenaki Indian ancestry. His many books for children include, most recently, *Sacajawea* and *Squanto's Journey*. He lives in Greenfield Center, New York.

Lisa Rowe Fraustino:

"In 1968, I was a very impressionable seven-year-old in what seemed an unstable, frightening world. Television was the newest technological breakthrough, and, like Jacket, I took to heart the stories on the nightly news narrated by Walter Cronkite, illustrated by black-and-white footage of assassinations, protests, and casualties in Vietnam. My fears of violence and loss led to a lifelong desire for peace—and a belief in the power of hope and love. These are the themes I tried to communicate in 'Things Happen.'"

Lisa Rowe Fraustino is the author of *Ash* and the editor

of *Dirty Laundry: Stories About Family Secrets,* both award-winning books for young adults. She teaches and lives with her three teenage children in northeastern Pennsylvania.

M. E. Kerr:
"When I was a teenager, my seventeen-year-old brother served in World War II, as so many young men did. There was only one conscientious objector in my hometown. He was part of a small group, followers of the Catholic pacifist Dorothy Day. He was sent to work at a mental institution, a real 'bedlam,' to serve without pay. His family suffered slurs written across the windows of their store, slights from towns-people, and the consensus they had raised a traitor. I never forgot him, nor the family.... This story is adapted from a novel about him, *Slap Your Sides.*"
M. E. Kerr lives in East Hampton, New York.

David Lubar:
"I have tons of stories on my hard drive—tales about every-thing from vampires and carnival monsters to fencing teams and fishing trips. But none of them are about war. So when the opportunity came to submit a war story to this collection, I had to start from scratch. As I was thinking about war, try-ing to dredge a great plot or situation from the scrap yard that serves as my brain, the phrase *War is swell* floated through my mind, a takeoff on the famous Civil War quote of General Sherman, *War is hell.* Rather than let it pass, I grabbed hold. (This is really the major trait that separates writers from

other folks. We preserve our weird thoughts.) Nice title. Now all I needed was a story to slip beneath it so it wouldn't fall to the bottom of the page. Okay—how could war be swell? *What if* (and that is a magic phrase every writer cherishes) there was someone whose situation was so bleak that it was improved by the spoils of war? What if...? From there, it was easy. The real magic is that each of us could take the seed of this *what if* and write an entirely different story. Mine was about Jorgi and Katya. I hope you liked it. If so, please feel free to sample some of my other writing, both stories and novels. I trust you are clever enough to know where to look."

David Lubar lives and writes in Nazareth, Pennsylvania.

Lois Metzger:

"Even a war without guns can destroy. This was the case during the Cold War, as it was called, the name for the continuing tension between the United States and Russia after World War II. Here at home, it was a time of suspicion, paranoia, betrayal, fear, and confusion, and tens of thousands of people were caught in the crossfire, their lives disrupted. This story, 'Snap, Crackle, Pop,' is based on the true story of a librarian, Mary Knowles, whose long ordeal received national attention in the 1950s."

Lois Metzger's novels for young adults include *Ellen's Case*, *Barry's Sister*, and *Missing Girls*. She has contributed to *The New York Times Book Review*, *The New Yorker*, and *The Nation*, among other periodicals. She and her husband, writer Tony Hiss, live with their son, Jacob, in New York City.

Gloria D. Miklowitz:

"I became steeped in Holocaust literature while growing up, reading *The Wall*, about the siege of the Warsaw ghetto, *Exodus*, about the effort of surviving Jews from the Holocaust to emigrate to Palestine, and many other books. Palestine was the only hope for these refugees from death camps. I wanted to live, through my characters, how that time felt."

Gloria D. Miklowitz's most recent books include *Secrets in the House of Delgado*, *Masada: The Last Fortress*, and *Past Forgiving*. She lives in La Cañada Flintridge, California.

Dian Curtis Regan:

Dian Curtis Regan lived in Puerto La Cruz, Venezuela, for three years, from 1998 to 2001. She experienced her share of unrest in the streets, electricity and water outages, and the lack of fat-free frozen yogurt. Still, she found local politics fascinating, and constantly squelched her urge to "fix" Venezuela. Dian offers special thanks to Sally Hefley, Donna Mitcha, Mary Rath, David Hefley, Daniel Hefley, Sam Robinson, and Iván Peña.

Dian is the author of forty books for young readers, including *Princess Nevermore*, *The Friendship of Milly and Tug*, and the *Monster of the Month Club* quartet. A native of Colorado, she has also lived in Texas and Oklahoma and presently lives in Kansas. Her Web site is www.diancurtisregan.com.

Graham Salisbury:

"Writing this story got me thinking. War. We hate it, but we do it. A lot. Why is it that we humans are such belligerent creatures? Why is it that when some car rips past us on the road, we think, What an idiot, what a stupid fool! instead of, He must have an injured kid lying on the backseat and needs to get to the hospital quickly? Why is it that when a checker at a grocery store stops to coo over some woman's baby while we fume in line behind her, we think, Good grief, get moving, what do you think this is, old-home week? instead of, Hey look, the baby-sitter brought the checker's baby in to say hello? Why is it that when the Japanese bombed Pearl Harbor, we thought, There are dirty spies everywhere, the Japanese among us can't be trusted, arrest them all! instead of, How I feel for my Japanese neighbors, how frightened they must be, just like me? Huh. War is in our hearts. Yup. Nowhere else. It's in our hearts."

Graham Salisbury's books include *Under the Blood-Red Sun* and *Lord of the Deep*. He lives in Portland, Oregon.

Marilyn Singer:
"I was a young adult during the Vietnam War period. The devastation—loss of lives, physical wounds, destruction of the environment—distressed me very much. It still does. But more recently I've been troubled by the devastation wreaked after the war ended—psychological scars, learning-disabled children affected by the chemicals their fathers were exposed to during battle, fractured families. Out of that concern came this story, 'Shattered.' Thanks to Elizabeth Konkle; Ernest, Ernie, and Becca Porcelli; Brad Walker; and Van Wolverton

for their help. I'm especially grateful to Jennifer Armstrong, who pestered me into writing this story."

Marilyn Singer is the author of over sixty books for children and teens. She has edited and contributed to two short-story anthologies: *Stay True: Short Stories for Strong Girls* and *I Believe in Water: Twelve Brushes with Religion.*

Suzanne Fisher Staples:

Suzanne Fisher Staples was an Asia-based reporter for United Press International in the 1970s and 1980s. She covered the first two years of the war in Afghanistan, which began in December 1979. She is the author of the Newbery Honor Book *Shabanu: Daughter of the Wind* and its sequel, *Haveli,* as well as *Dangerous Skies* and *Shiva's Fire.* She lives in Chattanooga, Tennessee, where she is at work on another novel.

Source Notes

The facts at the bottom of each story were gathered from the following sources:

(1) The Palestinian Refugee ResearchNet, run by McGill University (*www.arts.mcgill.ca/mepp/PRRN/proverview.html*).

(2) Victoria Sherrow, *Encyclopedia of Youth and War: Young People as Participants and Victims*. Phoenix: Oryx Press, 2000.

(3) Sherrow, *Encyclopedia of Youth and War*.
The Japanese American National Museum (*www.janm.org*).

(4) Cynthia Eller, *Conscientious Objectors and the Second World War: Moral and Religious Arguments in Support of Pacifism*. New York: Praeger, 1991.

(5) Thomas Omestad, "Revolutionary Appeal: Venezuela's Chavez Battles the Rich—and the Tide of History," *U.S. News & World Report*, June 11, 2001, 36–38.

(6) David Caute, *The Great Fear: The Anti-Communist Purge Under Truman and Eisenhower*. New York: Simon & Schuster, 1978.

(7) James Dickerson, *North to Canada: Men and Women Against the Vietnam War*. Westport, CT: Praeger, 1999.
David S. Surrey, *Choice of Conscience: Vietnam Era Military and Draft Resisters in Canada*. New York: Praeger, 1982.

(8) Sherrow, *Encyclopedia of Youth and War*.
Unicef, *The State of the World's Children 2001*
(*www.unicef.org/sowc01*).

(9) Laurence M. Hauptman, *Between Two Fires: American Indians in the Civil War*. New York: The Free Press, 1995.

(10) Ed Griffin-Nolan, *Witness for Peace: A Story of Resistance*. Louisville, KY: Knox Press, 1991.

(11) Unicef, *The State of the World's Children 2001*
(*www.unicef.org/sowc01*).

(12) Dr. Paul Valent, *Child Survivors: Adults Living with Childhood Trauma*. Australia: William Heinemann, 1994.